The CAPTAIN'S DOG

The CAPTAIN'S DOG

*My Journey
with the
Lewis and Clark
Tribe*

ROLAND SMITH

Gulliver Books
Harcourt Brace & Company
San Diego   New York   London

Acknowledgments

As always I want to thank my first readers—Melanie Gill, Mike Roydon, Marie Smith, Zach Teters, and Pat Washington—for their insightful comments. I would also like to thank my agent, Barbara Kouts, for arranging the lunch, all those years ago, where the seed for this book was first planted. And a very special thanks to my editor, Anne Davies, and her assistant, Nina Hess, for guiding me on this wonderful journey. This book is as much theirs as it is mine.

Gulliver Books is a registered trademark of Harcourt Brace & Company.

Library of Congress Cataloging-in-Publication Data
Smith, Roland, 1951–
The captain's dog: my journey with the Lewis and Clark tribe/Roland Smith
p.   cm.
"Gulliver Books."
Summary: Captain Meriwether Lewis's dog Seaman describes his experiences as he accompanies his master on the Lewis and Clark Expedition to explore the uncharted western wilderness.
ISBN 0-15-201989-8
1. Lewis and Clark Expedition (1804–1806)–Juvenile fiction. [1. Lewis and Clark Expedition (1804–1806)–Fiction. 2. Dogs–Fiction. 3. West (U.S.)–Discovery and exploration–Fiction. 4. Explorers–Fiction.]   I. Title.
PZ7.S657655Cap   1999
[Fic]–dc 21   99-25608

Designed by Linda Lockowitz
Text set in Cloister Old Style

C E F D B
Printed in the United States of America

For Marie,
the best partner an explorer ever had

SEAMAN'S JOURNEY WEST

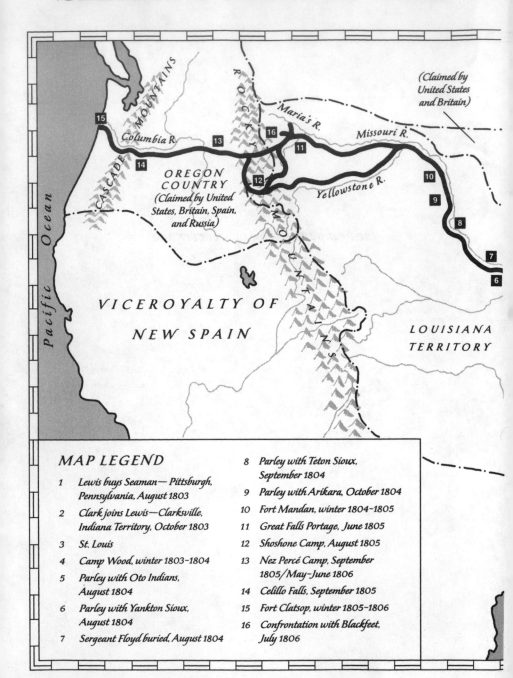

(Claimed by United States and Britain)

ROCKY MOUNTAINS

Maria's R.

Missouri R.

Columbia R.

Yellowstone R.

CASCADE MOUNTAINS

OREGON
COUNTRY
(Claimed by United
States, Britain, Spain,
and Russia)

ROCKY MOUNTAINS

Pacific Ocean

VICEROYALTY OF

NEW SPAIN

LOUISIANA
TERRITORY

15

13

16

11

14

12

10

9

8

7

6

MAP LEGEND

1 Lewis buys Seaman— Pittsburgh, Pennsylvania, August 1803

2 Clark joins Lewis—Clarksville, Indiana Territory, October 1803

3 St. Louis

4 Camp Wood, winter 1803–1804

5 Parley with Oto Indians, August 1804

6 Parley with Yankton Sioux, August 1804

7 Sergeant Floyd buried, August 1804

8 Parley with Teton Sioux, September 1804

9 Parley with Arikara, October 1804

10 Fort Mandan, winter 1804–1805

11 Great Falls Portage, June 1805

12 Shoshone Camp, August 1805

13 Nez Percé Camp, September 1805/May–June 1806

14 Celillo Falls, September 1805

15 Fort Clatsop, winter 1805–1806

16 Confrontation with Blackfeet, July 1806

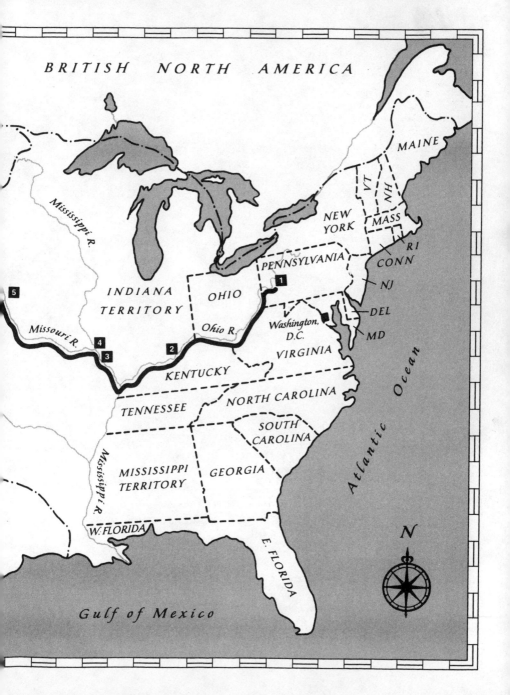

BRITISH NORTH AMERICA

MAINE

VT

NH

NEW
YORK

MASS

RI

CONN

PENNSYLVANIA

NJ

INDIANA
TERRITORY

OHIO

DEL

Washington,
D.C.

MD

Mississippi R.

Ohio R.

VIRGINIA

Missouri R.

KENTUCKY

Atlantic Ocean

TENNESSEE

NORTH CAROLINA

SOUTH
CAROLINA

Mississippi R.

MISSISSIPPI
TERRITORY

GEORGIA

W. FLORIDA

E. FLORIDA

N

Gulf of Mexico

1

2

3

4

5

1808

On a vast prairie east of the Rocky Mountains...

JOHN COLTER gallops into camp, jumps off his horse, and shouts, "Seaman? Good Lord! Is that really you? We thought you were dead!"

He falls to his knees in front of me and takes a handful of fur on either side of my face. He looks into my eyes, just like he used to, and makes that silly noise like a bull elk bugling for a cow.

Colter isn't alone. George Drouillard is with him. He swings off his horse and gives me a solid nod, which is about as emotional a greeting as I have ever seen him give.

Oh, it's good to see these men again!

Colter looks at Twisted Hair and grins. "When we rode up, Chief, I thought you had yourself a pet buffalo calf in camp!"

Twisted Hair doesn't understand a word Colter says, but he smiles at the white man's enthusiasm. Colter is dressed entirely in soiled buckskin except for his feet, which are shod in buffalo-hide moccasins. His face is burned as dark as the chief's and there are a few more creases than the last time I saw him. His brown hair hangs behind his head like a horse's tail, nearly brushing the ground as he kneels in front of me.

Drouillard is dressed in the same manner, but he hasn't changed much. He still looks like a large black bear dressed up as a deer.

Each has two horses with him. One to ride and one to carry the furs they've trapped and traded for. By the size of the piles, my old friends have been doing mighty well for themselves.

I look across the grassy plain beyond their horses, hoping the Captain is with them, wondering if he'll be happy or cross to see me. But he is not there. I am disappointed but not surprised.

Colter stands and pays his respects to Chief Twisted Hair and they begin speaking in hand-talk. Drouillard was always better at this language, but he lets Colter do the talking, and I see Colter's hand-talk has improved a good deal.

"We've come a long way to trade with you," Colter says.

Twisted Hair nods. "I must leave today to visit another camp. When I return we will trade. I will also bring people from the other camp to trade with you."

"How many days will you be gone?" Colter asks.

"Two days...three days at most. You can stay here while I'm gone and rest."

"Lord knows we could use some of that," Colter says to Drouillard.

Drouillard nods.

Later that night, after most of the Nez Percé have covered themselves with their robes, I lie near Colter and Drouillard's fire as I have done so many times before, listening to them talk. Their conversation is interrupted by the arrival of Mountain Dog and the old woman, Watkuweis. Mountain Dog is carrying the bag made from otter skin. Colter invites them to sit down.

"That's one beautiful bag," Colter says to Drouillard.

"Have you come to trade for your bag?" Drouillard asks Mountain Dog with hand-talk.

Mountain Dog shakes his head and looks at Watkuweis.

"We came here to show you something," Watkuweis says in French.

Drouillard and Colter stare at her in shock. French is Drouillard's boyhood tongue.

"I didn't know you spoke French," Drouillard says.

"Long ago I had a Frenchman for a husband and learned to speak his words."

"But you never told us this when—"

Watkuweis laughs. "Your chiefs never asked me. They just assumed none of us understood your words. I can read some of the French words, too." She takes the otter bag from Mountain Dog and opens it carefully, with the respect big medicine deserves. Inside is a small book with a red-leather cover and a brass clasp holding the book closed. "These words are not French. I believe they are in Colter's tongue."

She hands the book to Colter.

"Open it," Drouillard says.

Colter unhooks the clasp. He stares down at the first page, then looks up Watkuweis. "Lord Almighty! This belongs to Captain Lewis. It says right here it's his personal diary."

Watkuweis looks at Drouillard. "I want Colter to read the book to us."

"Where did Mountain Dog get this book?"

"I will tell you when the reading is finished. Colter will read the English, you will tell me the words in French, and I will pass the words to Mountain Dog in our language."

"What are you all jabbering about?" Colter asks.

"She wants you to read it."

"Out loud?"

"Yep. You read and I'll translate it into French as best I can."

Colter looks at Drouillard, nods, then scoots a little closer to the fire to better see the words in the flickering light. He begins to read....

May 23, 1804

At last we are all together and on our way with the immediate goal of following the Missouri River to the Mandan Indian village where we will spend the winter.

Our mission, given to us by President Jefferson, is to find and map the most direct navigable route to the Pacific Ocean—the long-sought-after Northwest Passage; make contact with the Indians along the way, with an eye toward setting up friendly trade between our nations; and observe and record the flora and fauna, terrain, Indian customs, and anything else that might help secure the future of our country. To this end, I, Captain Clark, and some of the other men are keeping official journals of our expedition, but this little red journal I start today will not be part of the official record.

As I make this first entry I am sitting on a high bluff above the Missouri with my dog, Seaman. It seems as if I have spent my entire life preparing for this journey. I feel ready for whatever we might encounter....

As John Colter speaks from the red book, my mind wanders back to that very day with Captain Lewis. I see him bend down to look at a delicate flower growing at the base of a hickory tree....

CAPTAIN LEWIS snipped the stem with his thumbnail, smelled it, held it up to the sunlight, then tasted one of the leaves. "Never seen anything like it," he said, carefully putting it into his plant press.

I sniffed the ground around the flower. A mouse had passed by early that morning. It was a female mouse with milk. I wanted to find her nest, but I didn't get the chance.

"Let's go, Sea," the Captain said, and he continued up the steep deer trail. Before leaving I lifted my hind leg and marked the hickory so other animals would know we had been there.

I caught up with the Captain and bounded ahead, stopping at a rocky bluff hundreds of feet above the Missouri River. As I sat waiting the sun came out from behind a cloud and warmed my thick black fur. I began panting to cool myself off.

The Captain walked up with long purposeful strides and stood beside me. "I see you found us a good spot, Sea." He scratched my head, the top of which just about came to his elbow when I sat.

We could see downriver for several miles. The

muddy Missouri meandered back and forth like an endless brown snake. We didn't know it at the time, but it would take us more than a year to reach the serpent's head.

We were less than two weeks into our journey, and the snake had already tried to kill us on several occasions. Captain Lewis predicted it would strike many more times before our exploring was over.

We were traveling against the current, and it was painfully slow going. Presently our tribe was made up of nearly fifty men, hand-picked and trained by Captains Lewis and Clark over the winter; two horses; and one Newfoundland dog—me.

Some of the men walked alongshore hunting, a couple rode the horses scouting ahead, and the rest pushed, yanked, and rowed the three boats carrying our supplies up that roaring river. I was thankful I was a dog, able to travel freely without a burden.

The two smaller canoe-like boats, called pirogues, rode high on the water and rowed reasonably well, even against the powerful spring current. The long keelboat was a different beast altogether. It drifted wildly in the current, smashing into hidden sandbars and submerged snags. The men swore it had a pact with the Missouri to cause their destruction. On good days we made ten miles in as many hours, but on many a day the keelboat's progress was measured only in yards.

"Like leading a dead draft horse," York described it.

The keelboat's twenty-two oars were pretty near useless in the torrential current, and so was the sail, as the wind seemed to blow in the wrong direction on most days. Because of this the men had to pull her upriver, walking along the shore, falling to their knees under the weight of the slippery tow ropes, hands sliced and shoulders rubbed raw by the rough hemp.

"It's like pushing a square boulder up a mountainside!" Private John Colter said one evening as the men tended their wounds and dried their clothes around the fire.

It was the keelboat that had brought Captain Lewis and me together. At the time we met, I was living with a man named Brady on a dilapidated barge moored at the Pittsburgh wharf.

My mother had whelped on a ship in the middle of the Atlantic Ocean during a terrible storm, the motion of which hastened our birth according to the ship's physician, who seemed to know more about canine ailments than the human kind. For helping my mother whelp, the doctor was given the pick of the litter. He did not pick me.

So my life began on the sea, and for the longest time I thought the world was made of bad-tasting water that men floated upon in wooden ships. It wasn't until I was four months old that I learned humans made their permanent homes on something they called land.

Our owner was a sailor named O'Malley. When the ship docked at the New York harbor, O'Malley stuffed us into a gunnysack and walked down the gangplank with my mother following him. As usual, being the runt of the litter, I was at the bottom of the pile, but this time my size worked to my advantage. There was a small tear in the corner of the sack, which allowed me to glimpse this new land-world before my squirming sisters and brothers.

We bounced by shouting men unloading cargo from ships, and passed wooden buildings with people pouring in and out the doors—some dressed in fine clothes, some dressed in rags, all of them in a great hurry, as if their captain had just called them to quarters. There were also tall four-legged creatures hooked to wheeled boxes guided by humans who were holding strings attached to the creatures' mouths. I caught snatches of conversations in English and French, heard other human languages I did not yet understand, and learned we were in a place called the United States of America.

Before we left the harbor O'Malley stopped. "Newfoundlands!" he said proudly, and dumped us out of the sack. "Best darn water dogs in the world. Just look at the size of their mother!"

A man held us up in the air and poked us with his dirty fingers.

"How much?"

"Five dollars."

"Ha! And for this one?" He pinched my ear. "He's half the size of the others."

"Five dollars," O'Malley insisted. "He's small, but smarter than all the other pups put together. I swear he sometimes knows exactly what I'm saying."

I knew what he was saying *all the time*. Dogs know humans better than they will ever know us. We are skilled watchers, and watching a human's face, posture, and hands is more than enough to pick up the gist of their meaning. Combining these signals with a human's tone of voice and the scents they send out makes any language perfectly understandable. After a couple days of watching and listening, a dog could talk the language back to them if our mouths worked that way. And it is a shame they don't, because we could teach humans a thing or two.

"I'll take both his brothers," the man said.

And back in the bag I went with my two sisters.

Later that night, after O'Malley had spent the ten dollars in a pub, he sold my two sisters to the barmaid for a bottle of whiskey and a handful of coins she had in her apron pocket. Having drunk the bottle of whiskey, O'Malley began to feel exceedingly lucky and got into a dice game with a group of men. On his first throw he lost the coins. On the second throw he lost my mother and me to an American riverman named Brady.

Brady sold my mother but kept me. "You'll be an easy keeper 'cause you're a runt. In fact, that's what I'm going to call you. Come on, Runt." It wasn't long before I outgrew this name.

When I met the Captain I had been with Brady for nearly a year as he hauled goods up and down rivers on his small barge. We had been docked in Pittsburgh for two weeks, waiting for a load, the afternoon Captain Meriwether Lewis arrived to check on the men building his keelboat. I liked the cut of his jib, as the sailors said. There was a ruggedness beneath his gentlemanly clothes. He was a tall handsome man with brown hair. His eyes were sharp and intelligent, with a hint of sadness he could not quite disguise.

I wanted to do something to cheer him up, so I dropped the big rat I had just killed at his feet. This must have left a good impression, because Captain Lewis marched right over to Brady's boat and said, "I want to buy this Newfoundland pup."

I was hardly a pup, being at the time fourteen months old, but I was impressed with his knowing an outstanding canine when he saw one. A skill Brady did not have.

"He's not for sale," Brady said, scratching his scraggly tobacco-stained beard. Just a week earlier, Brady had been complaining to his pals about the cost of feeding me and asked if any of them wanted to take me off his hands for free.

"I've been looking for a dog," Captain Lewis said. "Are you sure I can't convince you to sell him?"

"He's an awful good ratter. I'm going to keep him around."

Brady had no idea how good I was at catching rats, as he only let me off my rope a few minutes each day so I didn't foul his deck. I despised being tied up, but I always returned to the barge when Brady whistled. Not because I was fond of the man, but because I was afraid of the consequences if I didn't return. Brady had a terrible temper and was quick and accurate with the horse quirt he always carried—"to keep you obedient, Runt," as he so prettily put it.

"I'll give you five dollars for him," Captain Lewis said.

Brady laughed. "Even if he were for sale, I wouldn't part with him for such a paltry sum. A fine Newf like this...And smart? He does whatever I say."

"Ten dollars."

"Sir, you insult me."

"Fifteen."

Brady did not agree to the price, but he looked much less insulted. He told the Captain how he had traveled to Newfoundland personally, at great risk and expense, to pick me out of the litter. "Can't trust nobody for an important decision like that. Champion here cost me a fortune, but he was worth every penny."

So now my name was Champion. I liked it, but the name was not destined to last long.

"He saved me from drowning three times," Brady continued. "How can you put a price on that?"

I had not saved him once and I wasn't sure that I would if the opportunity arose.

It was clear that the Captain did not believe Brady for a second, but he reached into his purse and pulled out two ten-dollar gold pieces and bounced them in the palm of his hand, saying, "My absolute final offer is twenty dollars."

"Done!" Brady snatched the coins from the Captain's hand like a hungry gull after a minnow.

Captain Lewis got down on one knee and scratched me behind my ears. He seemed well pleased with the bargain. I hoped he remained that way.

"Now that he's yours, what do you plan to do with him?" Brady asked, more out of curiosity than concern.

"He'll be going to the Pacific Ocean with me and back."

Brady looked across the yard at the half-completed keelboat. "In that?"

The Captain nodded.

"With all due respect, sir, the craft you're building is not seaworthy. Not by a long shot. It will never round the Cape. You'll be lucky if it doesn't founder when the first ocean swell strikes it."

"I'm not going by sea," Captain Lewis said. "I'm

going down the Ohio, up the Mississippi and the Missouri, and from there—"

"Ah…so it's the Northwest Passage you're looking for."

The Captain nodded. "Among other things."

"They say there's nothing out in that wilderness but red savages, monstrous animals, and disease," Brady said, warming to his subject. "No one has ever—"

Captain Lewis ignored Brady and turned his full attention to me. "I'll call you Seaman," he said. "Before this is over you will have seen both the Atlantic and Pacific Oceans."

So I went from Runt to Champion to Seaman in the span of a few minutes.

"You'll be needing a rope to tie him up with," Brady said. "I have one on the barge."

"I will not need a rope. Let's go, Seaman."

After the keelboat was completed, we took it down the Ohio River to Clarksville in the Indiana Territory, where Captain William Clark joined us. Captain Clark was a red-headed man cut from the same sturdy material as Captain Lewis. Both men were hard muscled and six feet tall. They complemented each other in just about everything. Captain Clark was a better boatman than Captain Lewis. Captain Lewis was a better navigator. Captain Clark was a better mapmaker. Captain Lewis was a better botanist and biologist. Captain Clark took comfort in the company of men, talked easily with them, and enjoyed a good laugh. Captain Lewis was partial to solitude—a man of few words—but there was strength in those long silences. What one lacked the other had. Our tribe would have two chiefs, but they would lead as one.

From Clarksville we traveled up the Mississippi to Saint Louis and from there to Wood River, where we wintered with the men the captains had recruited along the way. In those days and the many that followed, the only rope the Captain needed was my devotion, and by the time we started up the Missouri he certainly had that.

That day sitting on the bluff was the first time I saw the red book. He pulled it out of his knapsack and started scratching words on the first page with that little spear he dipped in the black water he called ink. Sometimes he stopped scratching and looked down at the muddy river with a look of contentment. After an hour or so he closed the book and put it back in his knapsack.

"We better go and check on the men," he said, starting back down the trail to the river.

The winding trail was more like a ledge than a trail, not much wider than I was long. Below the ledge was a sheer drop of nearly two hundred feet. I ran ahead of the Captain, thinking that if I hurried I would have time to sniff around for that mouse near the hickory.

As I rounded the first bend I glanced back to see how far the Captain was behind me and saw the ledge he was walking on suddenly give way.

He disappeared from view. I was so stunned that for a moment I just stood there staring at the spot. When my wits returned I hurried over to the edge, expecting to see his broken body on the rocks below.

But Captain Lewis was alive! Somehow he had managed to pull the knife from his scabbard and stick the long blade into the cliff face to stop his fall. He was hanging about twenty feet below me, in a very precarious position. Gingerly he squirmed around until he found an outcrop with his moccasins and got his legs under him. He looked up and must have noticed the worry on my face, because he gave me a reassuring grin and said, "Everything's fine, Sea. With a little luck I'll be with you presently."

Using his knife, he clawed his way back and pulled himself up over the edge. He sat there for a few seconds, gathering himself. When he caught his breath, he said, "And that, my dear Sea, is why we have two captains on this journey."

June 12, 1804
The past few evenings we have been serenaded by nightin-
gales. Their song reminds me of my father. They were
singing that morning so many years ago when my father
came home on leave from the army and paid his final visit to
us. I remember feeling so intimidated and shy I could barely
utter a word in his presence. He was more than a man. It was
almost as if some god had entered our home.

The two days he stayed with us were wonderful, and
then he was off to his command. None of us could have
imagined that on his way there he and his horse would be
swept away crossing the Rivanna River. That his horse would
drown and that Father would return to us in a terrible condi-
tion, drenched from the river and a downpour of cold rain. I
remember Mother stripping off his clothes, putting him into
bed, and making him drink hot herbal tea. Despite her ef-
forts, he contracted pneumonia. I watched him shiver and
sweat for two days. And when he passed from us, I learned
that gods can die, too.

*We have taken on a man by the name of Pierre Dorion,
a trader who has lived among the Yankton Sioux for many
years. We were lucky to run across him. . . .*

"If you ask me, Dorion was lucky to run across us,"
Colter says. "Probably the luckiest day of his life.
How else would an old reprobate like him get to
meet the president of the United States?"

THE MEN WERE always talking about luck. It came in
two versions—good and bad. After a time I got a sense
of what they meant by this word and began to recognize
it myself. And the day Dorion arrived was a day of very
good luck for me.

I was on the trail of a buck, which took me up a tree-
covered hillside. When I reached the small clearing on
top I stopped my pursuit, realizing the buck was traveling too fast for me to catch up with him. I had just lain
down in the cool grass to catch my breath when I heard
Private Cruzatte call out from the river, "Boats ahead!"

Cruzatte was our one-eyed, fiddle-playing boatman.
He and Private Labiche were experienced rivermen who
had traveled the Missouri before and were therefore as-
signed to permanent duty on the keelboat. One of them
manned the stern paddle while the other hung over the
bow, pushing logs out of the way with an iron-tipped
pole and calling out what lay ahead.

A day or two before, we had encountered two boats with French trappers in them making their way down the Missouri to sell their furs. They had run out of powder and food. The captains gave them some of ours. But these pirogues that Cruzatte was hollering about had a different smell to them. The wind blew a scent up to me that made me drool. My paws moved beneath me like they had sprouted wings, and I flew down the hill a hundred times faster than I had come up it.

I burst through the trees, jumped a short bank, and landed onshore still running. The keelboat and pirogues were already tied up and the men were milling about, taking advantage of this unscheduled stop to lick their wounds. I ran directly for the source of that beautiful smell, which was coming from one of the newly arrived canoes. Standing next to it was an old man, and I guess I gave him quite a start, because when he saw me he reached for his rifle.

Fortunately, before he could get a bead on me, Drouillard stopped him and explained that I was Captain Lewis's dog. Pierre Dorion nearly laughed his gray-bearded face off at the revelation, then made a big fuss over me, never having seen a canine my size. He said he'd thought I was an angry black bear. When he finished scratching me all over, he reached into a bucket and gave me a handful of buffalo grease. It tasted even better than it smelled, and I thought happily of the meals to come when we reached the buffalos' feeding grounds.

Dorion and the captains spent several hours talking about what lay ahead, with Drouillard translating their words. It turned out that Dorion had lived with the Yankton Sioux for nearly twenty years and had a Yankton Sioux wife, and a son by her. Captain Lewis was delighted to hear this and asked if Dorion would accompany us upriver to help us talk to the Sioux.

"Part of our mission," Captain Lewis explained, "is to make friendly contact with all the tribes we meet along the way. We want to set up trading posts, which cannot succeed unless there is an atmosphere of peace. To this end we would like to send some of the Sioux chiefs to Washington to meet with President Jefferson."

Dorion thought he could arrange this, but he warned the captains that the Yanktons were just one branch of the Sioux nation and that farther up the Missouri we were going to run into their cousins, the Teton Sioux.

"And they, gentlemen, are a very different breed from the Yanktons," Dorion explained. "They are brigands and will try to stop you from going upriver, or at the very least charge you a heavy toll to pass safely."

"We don't want to make trouble," Captain Lewis said. "But we are prepared to stop trouble if need be."

The captains took Dorion to the keelboat and gave

him a demonstration of what they meant by this. Normally I didn't like these loud displays—the ruckus hurt my ears and made me jump. But I stuck next to Dorion all through it, hoping he might give me another handful of that delicious buffalo grease.

The keelboat had a thing on it called a swivel gun, which was a small cannon set on a stand that could be swung around in any direction. It could be loaded with a single lead ball weighing about a pound, or with several handfuls of musket balls. To fire the cannon off they lit a small candle called a taper, touched the flame to the charge, and *boom!* Branches blew off trees, and every animal within five miles stopped what it was doing. The boat also had two guns on board, called blunderbusses, which swung around and spit out noise and destruction of a smaller nature.

The captains fired each of these guns in turn for Dorion, and when they finished, Captain Lewis brought out his pride and joy—a rifle called an airgun that whispered when it was fired. Air was pumped inside the rifle and when he pulled the trigger, the ball came out with hardly a sound. The Captain loved this marvelous gun.

"Those will certainly make an impression on them," Dorion admitted after the white smoke cleared. "But your guns will have little affect on two hundred Teton warriors shooting arrows if they decide to take your goods away from you. They can notch their arrows much faster than you can charge your rifles. Do not underestimate any of the Indians you meet. Their ways are different from ours, but they are smart and they'll know that your guns and supplies would make them the most powerful tribe on the continent."

The captains exchanged worried glances—but I didn't hear what they had to say about Dorion's warning, because about that time Cruzatte broke out his fiddle and started making the squeaky noises that I liked less than the sound the swivel gun made. Though it meant parting from Dorion and his buffalo grease, I went for a ramble until the music stopped, which wasn't until late that night.

July 4, 1804
At sunset we celebrated our country's 28th birthday by firing the cannon and giving the men an extra ration of whiskey.

We still have not determined which of the men will become part of the permanent party and proceed west with us after we winter at the Mandan village. Some of the men have indispensable skills, others we are watching carefully to see what they can add to help our efforts....

DURING THE WINTER I'd grown very attached to this tribe of men and now considered them my family. I knew their moods, their sense (or lack) of humor, their sleeping habits, which foods they enjoyed and the foods they could not abide. I knew which of them were the best marksmen, and which if separated from the tribe would perish for lack of skill.

As we made our way upriver my role within the tribe became clearer to me. I could not paddle or pull the boat, cook meals, or play the fiddle, but I had other talents that were just as useful.

I had discovered long ago that human beings have pitiful noses. About all they can do is breathe through them, which is a shame and a great handicap in the wilderness. If the wind is blowing right, my nose can smell a deer two miles away and a skunk a considerable distance farther. I can tell the future with my nose and sometimes figure out what happened a day or two before if the scent is strong.

Another almost useless appendage is the human ear. The men couldn't hear anything until it was right in front of them, and sometimes not even then. My ears work in concert with my nose. I can conjure a pretty clear picture of what lies ahead long before I get to it or it gets to me.

These skills came in pretty handy during our journey, although conveying what I knew without the use of words was a challenge at times. Every night the captains posted sentries to forewarn us if we came under attack. This was not the men's favorite duty, but I didn't mind it, so whenever I could muster the energy I spent my nights patrolling the camp.

If I heard or scented something unusual, aside from the men snoring and breaking wind, I'd low-growl, and if that didn't rouse the men from their sleep, I would let out a series of deep barks. This got everyone swearing and stumbling around in a hurry, which was great fun to see, but I was careful not to use this alarm unless there was good cause.

A few nights before the men's big celebration, I'd learned that trouble didn't always come from outside the camp. That night I saw Private Collins tap a whiskey barrel after the other men had gone to sleep. He held his tin cup under the spigot two or three times and after a while he started to sing and sway. Pretty soon he was joined by Private Hall, and it wasn't long before their singing woke Sergeant Ordway, who changed their tune.

The next morning the captains held a court-martial. All the men participated in these trials, passing judgment as a group after hearing the facts. In this case the men were not inclined to forgive Collins and Hall, as the whiskey they drank belonged to everyone and the two men's taking more than their share meant the others would get less.

"Guilty!" The men shouted after hearing Collins's and Hall's side of the story. The punishment—one hundred lashes for Private Collins and fifty for Private Hall—commenced immediately, starting with Collins.

The lash was made out of strips of leather and when applied to a man's bare back, it opened up long bloody cuts, which took weeks to heal. Collins's shirt was removed, his arms tied around a tree, and he was whipped, with all the men counting each stroke out loud until they reached... *one hundred*!

Which was a relief to all of them. Collins did not hear the final call, as he had passed out on the fifty-second lash. Two men untied him and took him down to the river to clean and dress his wounds. Hall was next.

As soon as the punishment was completed, camp was broken and the boats were loaded. Privates Collins and Hall were expected to pull their oars on the keel-boat as usual.

July 10, 1804
If the number of furs we have seen coming downriver is any
indication, this country's bounty is endless. I am confident we
will prevail and find the Northwest Passage. With the discov-
ery of the passage we will be able to move these trade goods
easily from the Pacific to the Atlantic and beyond to other
countries by ship, greatly increasing our nation's commerce.

The scenery here is beautiful, but we are greatly
afflicted by the heat and mosquitoes. The men are fatigued
and several have boils on their skin. Private Joseph Fields
was bitten by a rattlesnake a few days back. I treated the
wound with a poultice of Peruvian bark. I think he will be
fine. The snake was killed and I put the skin and rattle in
my collection. Despite the afflictions the men seem to be in
good cheer. . . .

THE MISSOURI'S current lowered and slowed a little
more each day, which allowed us to increase our speed

up the river. The men's muscles were as hard as rocks and their skill at handling the boats had increased a hundredfold since we left Wood River in May. On some days we made better than twenty-five miles. Despite this, the men were not always in "good cheer," as Captain Lewis said.

The French voyagers, hired to take our two pirogues as far as the Mandan village, were constantly complaining about the pace the captains had set, and about the food. They were used to stopping several times a day to rest and eat. The captains rarely allowed any stops, except to make camp at night. The other men complained, too, but not as often, and not in the captains' presence. They were soldiers and this was not allowed.

I noticed that within our tribe were smaller tribes. This was most easily seen by how the men clustered themselves at night. The captains usually slept in or near the keelboat. The French voyagers slept near the red-and-white pirogues. The three sergeants—Floyd, Ordway, and Pryor—camped together near their men. The privates, Drouillard, and Dorion pretty much stayed together in a big group. And York, the tribe's only black man, put his bedroll within earshot of the captains, although he sometimes visited the privates in the evenings, after Captain Clark's needs had been tended to.

York was a big man, kind to everyone, even to those who were not kind to him. When treated unfairly, he responded with a smile rather than his fists, but I some-times smelled fury beneath that easy smile of his. It rose to the surface every time a man made a negative comment about his color, but he had learned to hold that angry flame inside and quench it with the juice deep in his belly.

The men claimed that York was Captain Clark's *slave,* and that this meant Captain Clark *owned* him. At first I did not believe them, but over the months I saw that it was true. I had more freedom to do as I pleased than he did.

As we got farther west, I saw slaves among the Indian tribes, too. These poor Indian slaves, mostly women and children, were captured in raids and bartered back and forth like the cows I had seen in stockyards when I was with Brady. I wondered if Captain Clark had raided York's tribe and taken him away from his people. However it had happened, York never complained about it, and although he had ample opportunity, he never tried to escape.

I moved freely among all these clusters of men, but there was one man I treaded lightly around. His name was Private Moses Reed. Some of the men called him a weasel, but to me that was an insult to the sleek beauty of the real animal. Moses Reed was slippery and mean-spirited. More like an eel than a weasel.

He was constantly shirking his duties and saying

bad things about the captains and sergeants when they were out of earshot. One day when no one was looking he kicked me in the ribs as hard as he could, and said, "I'll be eating you one day soon, you dumb mongrel! Mark my words."

There were other kicks, and sometimes Reed would seek me out, step on my toes, then curse me in front of the other men.

"The mongrel is always underfoot! He's a hazard to the entire expedition. What kind of captain would bring a giant dog along with him? He'll get all the food and we'll starve. Mark my words!"

Everyone had learned to ignore Reed's braying, except for Private John Newman, who followed Reed around like York followed Captain Clark. At night Reed and Newman slept a little off from the others so they could talk without anyone hearing them. One night as I patrolled the camp I heard them whispering.

"I been thinkin' about Dorion and those other trappers we've seen coming downriver," Reed said. "They must've had a thousand dollars' worth of skins in their dugouts. A thousand dollars' worth! One of them told me it only took them about two weeks to trap and trade for all them skins. He said the Indians have no idea what the furs are worth. You give them a couple worthless beads and they hand over a pile of beaver skins worth a fortune. Imagine making a thousand dollars in two weeks!"

"That's a lot of money, all right," Newman admitted.

"Instead of breaking our backs getting these boats upriver, we could be out trapping, just like them. In a year we'd be rich!"

"But we wouldn't get the land grant the army promised us for volunteering for the Corps. Four hundred acres is a lot of property."

"Yeah, if you want to be a farmer!" Reed snorted. "That's not for me, I tell you. Besides, we'll never see one acre of that land."

"What are you talking about?"

"The land deal was just a carrot they put out in front of us so we would agree to go."

"Not true!"

Reed laughed. "You're about as green as they come, Newman! I been in this army a lot longer than you and I know how it works. Mark my words."

Newman thought about this for a few moments. "If you knew they weren't going to give you the land, why did you volunteer?"

"Free trip into the interior," Reed said. "All paid for by the army. How else would I get a chance to see what's here? And now that I've seen it I can tell you I'm not going to wait two or three years to get at it."

"Desertion?"

"I didn't say that," Reed whispered quickly, and

changed the subject. "What about the girl you got waiting back home for you?"

"What about her?"

"Think she'll wait two years for you to come back?"

"I hope so. Said she would."

"Any other young men back home she might be interested in?"

Newman didn't answer.

"I thought so! How do you think she'd feel if you came back a lot sooner, with your pouch filled with money?"

"She'd be mighty happy," Newman said.

At that moment I wanted to drag Newman away from Reed and shake him, like my mother used to do to me when I was about to get myself into trouble. I took a step toward them.

"What's that?" Newman sat up suddenly.

"The Captain's dog. I'll fix him." Reed picked up a rock and threw it at me. He missed.

August 1, 1804

*We came across an Oto Indian a few days ago. He told us
that most of the Otos were out on the prairie, hunting buffalo, but claimed some others were not far from here. We sent
a man with the Indian to invite them to parley with us.*

*We continue to be plagued by various ailments. Last
night Captain Clark lanced a boil on one of the men and a
pint of pus was taken from the wound. Private Whitehouse
cut his knee with his knife and lost a great deal of blood, but
we managed to stem the flow. Sergeant Floyd has had a bad
cold for several days and some stomach problems, which I am
treating.*

*I have been virtually free of dark moods, and my
strength and health have been good as have Captain Clark's.
He is 34 years old today. For his birthday dinner he has
requested a saddle of fat venison, roasted beaver tail, and
elk steak, and for dessert some of the berries growing so
profusely around here.*

The men are clearly feeling the effects of their labors.
We will rest here a few days and wait for the Otos. We hope
this will give the men a chance to recover their strength....

CAPTAIN LEWIS calculated that each man was eating nine pounds of meat a day, and yet some of them were still going to sleep hungry. One night Drouillard came back to camp with an elk, Private Reubin Field came in with two deer, and John Colter brought in two beavers with fat tails, but this was barely enough food to feed the camp for one day.

This dearth of meat did not affect me, because there were certain parts of the animals the men refused to eat. They threw out piles of perfectly good food, entrails mostly, that were more than enough to slake my appetite. But the meat I was really looking forward to getting my teeth into was that buffalo animal's. The men were constantly talking about this beast, but only a handful of them had actually seen one. Every time I heard the word *buffalo,* drool spilled out of my mouth.

"Ready to ramble to the top of the bluff?" Captain Clark asked.

"I am." Captain Lewis put his pen down and closed the red book. "Let's go, Sea."

I ran ahead of them. As I neared the top I scented

something unfamiliar. I stopped and tried to get a sense of what this new smell meant, but no picture came to mind. The captains caught up with me and we stepped through an opening in the brush.

We were stunned by what we saw. I managed a low growl, but the captains were speechless for a moment or two. I hadn't seen an open area this big since I was a pup aboard ship. Before us was an ocean of golden grass stretching as far as we could see. The wind moved the long grass back and forth across the endless flat plain in long rolling waves.

"Prairie," Captain Clark said. "I had no idea it was so..." He couldn't seem to find the right word.

"Vast," Captain Lewis said.

For several minutes we just stood there staring at the stark, lonely beauty of it. All day long we had fought the river, not knowing this lay just above us. We walked about a mile across the grassy plain to a small stand of trees.

"Caw! Caw! Caw!"

A crow scolded us from the branch of one of the trees. I had seen hundreds of crows and ravens, but never one like this. On his left wing was a patch of feathers as white as a scrubbed mainsail.

"Caw! Caw! Caw!"

The captains were so used to hearing crows they didn't even bother to look up at it. I barked, trying to get their attention on the bird. If Captain Lewis saw it, he would certainly want to add it to his animal collection. He glanced up at the tree, then back across the prairie. I barked again.

"Quiet, Sea!" Captain Lewis said. "What's gotten into you?"

I guessed he had seen crows with white feathers on their wings before and was not interested in collecting this one. He would not have been able to shoot it anyway, because the next time I looked, the crow had vanished.

On our way back across the prairie I came across several new scents I was eager to investigate, but they had to wait because Captain Clark wanted to get back to camp and see how the men were doing with his birthday feast.

When we arrived Private Joseph Fields ran up to us. He was carrying a brownish gray animal about the size of a cat. Joseph and his older brother, Reubin, were both good hunters. Because of his excitement, I wondered if the animal he was holding was one of the buffalo we were all so eager to see, but one sniff of its musky carcass told me it wasn't.

"I shot it near a stream that runs into the river up ahead," Joseph explained. "It put up quite a ruckus—growling and carrying on. It had no idea what a rifle was. Didn't back off an inch when I pointed the barrel at it. What do you think it is, Captain Lewis?"

"I don't know." Captain Lewis laid the animal on the ground and examined it closely.

One of the French boatmen came over. "It's what we call a badger."

The creature seemed to make Captain Lewis happy, which did not go unnoticed by the men. From that day on all of them were on the lookout for new animals and plants to bring the Captain.

After Captain Lewis had eaten and participated in the birthday festivities, he quietly slipped away to the keelboat. In the dim lantern light he measured, skinned, and tanned the badger, writing down notes—like how many teeth it had—in the official journal he and Captain Clark were keeping. He offered me some of the meat from the carcass, but I didn't like it. It tasted sour. He threw the meat into the river but kept some of the badger's bones and its skull. He then took the still-wet skin and sewed it back together again, stuffing the body with cotton. I was to see him do this many times with different animals during the course of our journey, but I never understood the purpose. The results were much less satisfactory than the original animal had been.

For two days we stayed at this camp, which the captains named Council Bluff in anticipation of the parley we were to have with the Otos there. I used the time to take several rambles across the prairie to investigate the grass sea. My most interesting discovery was a small wild dog. I found the den where she had whelped, and a mile later I found her—a sleek, buff-colored beauty with long pointed ears and a bushy tail—and her two young ones. She caught wind of me as I approached, and she and her pups disappeared into the tall grass, which matched the color of their fur. I gave chase, but they were too quick, and I soon lost sight of them. I would not have done her any harm. I wished she had stayed around long enough to learn my intentions.

August 2, 1804
*This evening we were visited by a group of natives and a
French trapper who is living with them. They said they are
part of a band of about 250 Oto and Missouri Indians.
Their main chief, a man called Little Thief, is away hunting buffalo, but they said that several lesser chiefs are in the
area. We have invited them to parley with us tomorrow
morning....*

THE MEN WERE excited at the prospect of meeting their
first large group of Indians. They were also nervous and
made sure all the guns were loaded and ready in case
there was trouble. That night extra sentries were posted
around camp, but we didn't need them, as most of the
men were too anxious to sleep.

In the morning the men were up before the sun rose,
donning their best uniforms and getting ready for the
parley.

Captain Lewis spent most of the morning writing down what he was going to say to the Otos. A "speech," he called it. After he had scratched the words down he sat by himself and said them out loud, even though there was no one to hear him but me.

Captain Clark broke out a bundle filled with gifts for the Otos. Inside the bundle were red leggings, fancy dress coats, blue blankets, flags, beads, small looking glasses, and medals with President Thomas Jefferson's likeness stamped on them.

Not long after the sun melted the morning fog, about a hundred Otos walked into camp, led by a half dozen chiefs. It looked like they had gotten dressed up for the occasion as well. Our men fixed up the mainsail of the keelboat as an awning to protect the delegation from the hot sun.

When everyone was settled in, the sergeants had the men march with their rifles. It was an impressive display, with all their legs moving in unison like a centipede's, turning right and left at the sound of Sergeant Ordway's booming voice.

"Company, halt!" Ordway shouted. "Present arms!" The rifles were raised to their shoulders. "Fire!"

This got a jump out of the Otos. Next Captain Lewis fired his air rifle, which astonished them even more.

"And this," he said, "makes things appear closer." He handed one of the chiefs a brass tube. I had seen similar instruments when I was aboard the ship. "Hold it up to your eye."

The chief peered through the tube and let out a startled cry. "It turns my sight into eagle eyes," he said to Dorion, who was translating.

"Yes," Captain Lewis said. "And we have even greater magic than this."

He gathered the Otos around him and began reading his speech.

"Children…we have been sent by the great Chief of the seventeen nations of America to inform you that a great council was held between your old fathers, the French and Spaniards…"

He went on to tell them that the French and Spaniards, with whom the Otos had traded for many years, had returned to their homes across the sea and would never come back, and that President Thomas Jefferson was now their new father. I wasn't quite sure what Captain Lewis meant by all of this. It seemed important and I tried to pay close attention, but all I could think was that I wished the mosquitoes, who were out in great numbers, would return to their homes and never come back.

"The president is your only father; he is the only friend to whom you can now look for protection, or from whom you can ask favors, or receive good counsel, and he will take care to serve you, and not deceive you…"

Drouillard and Dorion did the best they could to try to translate these words with hand-talk, but I could see it was somewhat difficult for them.

"Children, our great Chief has sent us out here to clear the road, remove every obstruction, and make it the road of peace between himself and his red children who live here. He wants to know what you want. When we return we will tell him your desires, and they will be satisfied..."

He told them to stop warring among themselves and not to make war on the white tribe when they came to trade.

"If you make war on our people, you will bring upon yourselves the displeasure of your great father, who has the power to consume you as the fire consumes the grass of the plains. If you displease him, he will also stop all traders from coming up the river..."

The speech went on for some time, but at last Captain Lewis concluded and with Captain Clark began to hand out gifts to the chiefs. I could tell the chiefs were a little disappointed at the gifts, but they were too polite to complain. They got together and delivered a speech of their own, saying that they wanted to be friendly and that they could also use some gunpowder and whiskey. Captain Lewis obliged them by giving them a casket of powder, fifty balls, and a bottle of whiskey, and the chiefs left with a promise to send Little Thief to the captains as soon as he returned from hunting.

Overall the captains seemed quite pleased with how the parley went. After the Otos departed, Captain Lewis gathered the men and complimented them on their conduct. "I venture to say that if all of our councils go like this, President Jefferson will be well pleased with our success."

Then, as the captains were fond of saying, we proceeded on.

That evening at our new camp I was lying at Captain Lewis's feet as he scratched in the red book, and I was just about to doze off when I smelled Private Moses Reed approaching. My eyes snapped open and I stifled a growl before it left my throat. Captain Lewis did not tolerate my growling at the men, even men like Private Reed.

"Captain Lewis, sir?"

The Captain was so engrossed in the red book he had not seen Reed walk up, and was startled at the sound of Reed's voice. He looked up angrily. "What is it, Reed?"

"I left my knife at Council Bluff. I'd like to go back and fetch it."

Captain Lewis took a deep breath. "Yes, go ahead, but in the future be more careful. We can't be leaving our tools strewn all over the countryside."

"Yes, sir."

"And don't dawdle. I want you back before we leave tomorrow morning."

"Yes, sir. I'll be back bright and early."

I knew Private Moses Reed had not left his knife at Council Bluff. An hour earlier I had seen him carve his initials in a tree trunk with his knife.

August 11, 1804
Private Moses Reed has not returned from Council Bluff.
Captain Clark and I are certain that he has deserted—one of
our worst fears. We have sent Drouillard, Reubin Fields, and
several other men to apprehend him, with orders to put him
to death if he resists.

   The search party will also make contact with the Otos
again and see if Little Thief has returned from hunting
buffalo.

   This afternoon we walked up to an abandoned Omaha
village above the river. Dorion told us that smallpox killed
all the inhabitants....

"THE OMAHA were once a thriving nation," Dorion said
to Captain Lewis as they surveyed the village. "Along
with our trinkets we carried disease. Didn't turn out to
be a very good trade for them, did it?"

   The men poked around the ruins. Scattered inside

the crumbling earth-mound lodges were woven baskets, grinding stones, arrowheads, and old skins stiffened by weather and neglect. Dorion pointed out a large mound with an eight-foot pole in the middle of it. He said an Omaha chief called Black Bird was buried there, mounted on his horse. The men attached an American flag to the pole.

On the outskirts of the village I picked up the scent of the skittish canine from Council Bluff. Her trail led me all the way back to our previous camp, where I discovered she and her pups had been feeding on our left-over food scraps. This time, though she didn't let me too near, she did not run away. I settled down to eat some scraps myself and to enjoy her company.

The following afternoon, as I rode with the Captain in the keelboat, the wild dog appeared on the bank and barked at us. The little fool!

"What is it?" Captain Clark asked.

"Too small for a gray wolf," Captain Lewis said. "Must be a prairie wolf—the gray's little cousin. Are those pups with her? Row the boat over so we can take a closer look."

The two pups were about twenty yards in back of her, huddled near some bushes. As we approached she turned and made a noise at them. They skedaddled, but she stayed right where she was.

The captains grabbed their rifles with the intention

of putting her in the collection. I could not allow that. I jumped into the water and began barking at her.

"No, Sea!" the Captain shouted.

I pretended I didn't hear him and continued barking and swimming toward her. This finally got her moving, but it didn't prevent the captains from firing their rifles. Fortunately they both missed. Captain Lewis was cross with me for the rest of the day.

August 15, 1804
Fish Camp. The course of the river has started to loop back
on itself. On the 12th we made 18¾ miles by boat. After we
set up camp that evening I sent a man on foot back to our
previous camp, and he reported it was a mere 974 yards away
by land.

We have decided to stay here a few days to await the
arrival of Drouillard and the other men. I do hope they have
had success in apprehending Private Reed.

Captain Clark and some of the men constructed a net
out of willow bark. They dragged this trap down the stream
and caught nearly 800 fish....

I WAS NOT particularly fond of the fish the men were
eating. I managed to snap up a couple mice, but this was
not nearly enough to cure my hunger. By the second
morning at Fish Camp I was near to starving and
started thinking about all the meat we had left at the

previous camp, which was only a few miles away. I also started thinking about that pretty little prairie wolf. I regretted not getting to know her better and wondered if she was still feeding at our abandoned camps.

An exhausted Private Labiche arrived at Fish Camp that evening. "We caught that scoundrel, Reed," he told the captains. "Drouillard and the others are about ten miles back and will bring him in tomorrow morning."

"What about Little Thief?" Captain Lewis asked.

"He'll be here, too, along with a couple other chiefs."

I was hoping that Reed had escaped or that he'd been shot by Drouillard.

"York, bring Labiche some fish," Captain Clark said. "Labiche, you've earned some rest. We'll send someone out early tomorrow to meet them and show them where we're camped."

That someone was Joseph Fields, and when he set off the next morning I went with him. I was none too eager to see Reed again, but I wanted to get my teeth into some of the meat we had left behind. And I was hoping I might run into my prairie wolf as well.

When we were about parallel with our previous camp, the crow with the white feathers called down to me from a tree. Joe continued walking without so much as a glance up at it. White Feather flew in the direction of our old camp, and I followed. When I got to the camp, the crow was nowhere to be seen, but I did find some old meat to fill my belly. When I finished eating, I sniffed around and picked up the scent of my little prairie wolf who had been feeding on our leavings. And there was another scent as well—canine to be sure, but a different type from the prairie wolf. I followed this new scent confidently to the other side of the spit of land, which led me to another of our old camps.

When I got there, my bold confidence faded pretty quickly. The canines were gray wolves. The men had talked about these grays, but this was the first time I had seen them up close. They were three times bigger than the prairie wolf and there were nine of them in a circle around a pile of our old meat.

At first they didn't notice me, because they were too busy snarling at each other over the food. I thought about sneaking off, but just as I was about to back away, the biggest wolf perked his ears up and looked in my direction. I was bigger than he was, but I knew I wasn't a match for the whole pack. The big wolf and I locked eyes. I knew better than to turn tail and run. That would just get them excited and they would be on me faster than a falcon on a rabbit. I stood my ground, though my legs wanted to jump.

The big male made an odd sound deep in his throat and stood up. The other wolves stopped eating and followed suit. He moved toward me on stiff legs, with his tail standing straight up like a flagpole. This was not a good sign—something I had learned from dogs on wharves along the Ohio. The other wolves followed a step or two behind him.

I allowed him to get within about five feet before letting out my best warning growl. He stopped in his tracks, which I was gratified to see, but some of the other wolves slunk around behind me. They kept their distance, but it was impossible to keep an eye on all of them at once, surrounded as I was. At that moment I wished I had wings! One of the wolves darted in behind me. I reeled around to face him, and another wolf came in from my rear. I whipped around again. There was only one thing to do.

I snapped at the smallest of the wolves, a young female. My vigor disrupted the circle, and in that second I dashed through the opening.

The pack pursued me. I knew that if I stopped or hesitated I was doomed. My stamina was as good as any wolf's in the pack, but they were faster and accustomed to pursuing game. They lunged at my flanks and snapped at my hind legs, trying to cripple me. The leader managed to get in front of me and went for my nose. I lowered my head and bulled him over.

After a mile, two of the wolves dropped back, but the others were still right on my tail. I felt my legs begin to fail. I was going to have to stop and rest. I put on a burst of speed and pulled away from them, hoping to find a place I could put my tail against without them worrying me from behind, but there was no such place! They were going to take me in the open. Just as my legs started to go, I heard—

"Caw! Caw! Caw!"

White Feather swooped down upon us. At the time I wasn't certain if he was trying to help the wolves or hinder them, but his sudden appearance caused the leader to stumble, which threw the other wolves off the chase for a moment. And a moment was all I needed, because the next thing I heard were men's voices.

It was the Fields brothers.

"Caw! Caw! Caw!"

White Feather flew right to them, and my weak legs followed without breaking stride.

Startled at my sudden arrival, a couple of the Otos raised their war axes.

"Friend!" Drouillard shouted. "Friend! It's the Captain's dog."

I turned around, but the wolves were nowhere to be seen. Nor was White Feather.

"I wondered where you'd got off to," Joe said. "If I came back without you, the Captain would hang me along with our friend here."

I looked at Reed, as pleased as I ever would be to see

him, but it was clear he didn't feel the same way about me. His hands were tied behind his back and he looked as if he had been towed through a dry streambed.

As soon as we got back to camp, the court-martial commenced. Reed pleaded guilty to desertion and stealing a rifle, a shot pouch, powder, and balls. He was convicted and sentenced to run the gauntlet four times. He was also discharged from the permanent party. And for the rest of the summer he would travel in one of the pirogues with the French voyagers, with whom he would be sent back to Saint Louis in the spring. I was glad to hear this, as I wouldn't have to put up with him after that.

Captain Lewis, through Drouillard, explained the punishment to Little Thief and the other chiefs. "The men will form two lines facing each other, holding sticks. Private Reed will run this gauntlet four times while the men beat him with the sticks."

The chiefs were offended at the severity of the punishment and asked that Reed be pardoned. The captains stepped off by themselves to discuss the request.

"If we let him off this early in our journey," Captain Clark said, "I'm afraid it will set a poor example for the other men."

Captain Lewis nodded. "We are in for even harder times ahead. We must maintain discipline."

They walked back over to the chiefs and Drouillard.

"Tell the chiefs that desertion is our most serious offense," Captain Lewis said, so all the men could hear. "By his desertion Private Reed has not only jeopardized this expedition and wasted valuable time, he has also betrayed his fellow soldiers. Under our laws we could hang or shoot him for this. Running the gauntlet is the smallest penalty we can impose under the circumstances."

Little Thief and the other chiefs seemed to accept this. The men lined up in two rows.

I disliked Moses Reed, but watching him run the gauntlet was horrible. After his first time through, I slipped away, but I stayed within running distance of camp in case I met up with that pack of wolves.

August 19, 1804
After meeting with Chief Little Thief we are proceeding on.
Reed is in the white pirogue, no doubt suffering greatly.
Although he deserved every stroke, I still feel some measure
of pity for him.

At the moment my greatest concern is Sergeant
Charles Floyd, who is gravely ill. I am in the keelboat
at his side as I write this. Captain Clark spent the
entire night tending him and I am now doing what
I can. He has a great deal of pain in his stomach
region and all our attempts to relieve him have
failed....

THROUGHOUT OUR journey all the men suffered from various stomach ailments, but it was clear that Sergeant Floyd's sickness was something worse than a common bellyache.

Captain Lewis came out of the cabin and told the men to row the keelboat to shore.

"Start a fire and heat some water. I want to give Sergeant Floyd a warm bath to see if it will help him."

Captain Clark and York carried Floyd to shore and laid him next to the fire. "You'll be just fine," Captain Clark told him.

"I don't think so, Captain," Floyd said weakly. "I am going away. I want you to write a letter."

Before Captain Clark could get his writing things, Sergeant Floyd closed his eyes for the last time.

Above the shore was a high bluff. The men carried Floyd's body to the top, dug a deep hole, and lowered him into it. Captain Lewis read from his Bible and the men bowed their heads and prayed. When they finished filling the hole, Colter brought a piece of wood over to the mound to mark it.

"What should I write?" he asked the Captain.

"Something simple," Captain Lewis said sadly. "'Charles Floyd died here, 20 August 1804.'"

Not far from the bluff was a small river, which the captains named Floyd's River in honor of the sergeant. A vote was held and the men elected Private Patrick Gass to take Floyd's place as sergeant.

The men were all affected by Floyd's death, but

none more than Captain Lewis, who blamed himself for the sergeant's passing.

"There must have been something I could have done to save him," he said to Captain Clark.

"You did all that you could, Meriwether."

The Captain did not believe it was enough.

August 23, 1804
After our recent loss, the men have been much out of spirits.
But today we have something to celebrate—we shot our
first buffalo....

Colter looks up from the red book. "Remember when I killed that buff? That cheered us some."

"I killed the first buff," Drouillard says.

"In your dreams, partner. I remember that day clearly..."

It was neither of them.

JOE FIELDS ran into camp, shouting, "I killed me a buffalo! It's a huge beast!"

There was no one more cheered by this news than me. The captains sent a dozen men out onto the prairie to help Joe bring the meat back to camp, and every one of them was needed.

The buffalo was covered in woolly brown fur. It had a hump on its back, stubby horns, bulging brown eyes, and a beard, and it tasted better than anything I had ever had in my mouth. When we had all feasted to our satisfaction, the captains had the men cut the leftover meat into thin strips, salt them, then lay them in the sun to dry. They called this jerking. The dried meat was light to carry and didn't spoil.

Despite having their bellies filled with buffalo, some of the men were still dispirited by the loss of Sergeant Floyd. Those closest to the sergeant, including the captains, seemed to be spending more time on their own than they had prior to his passing. In the evenings when the work was done, they would wander off and find a spot away from the others and sit for long periods of time preoccupied with their thoughts.

August 27, 1804
Private Shannon did not come back to camp last night, and
we are greatly worried about him. We don't know if he's lost,
had trouble with Indians, or has met with some accident.
Reed's desertion, Floyd's death, and now the disappearance
of the youngest member of the party…

SHANNON WAS NOT a good hunter, and the Captain
was afraid that he might starve to death if they didn't
find him quickly. John Colter was sent out to look for
him, but he came back without picking up his trail.
Drouillard tried next, but he didn't have any luck,
either.

I started sniffing around and came to the conclu-
sion that they were searching in the wrong direction.
Shannon wasn't behind us. He was in front of us. He
must have missed our camp and thought that we were
ahead of him.

When I made the discovery the captains were both aboard the keelboat. I tried to get one of the men walking onshore to follow me, but they were tired and hungry and in no mood to pay attention.

"Quit pestering me!"

"Shut up, Sea!"

"Not now, you big skunk."

Humans can be so dense at times! Even if I had gotten them to follow me, they probably would not have understood what I was trying to show them. I had found Shannon's moccasin prints and a dead fire where he had roasted a small rabbit. The captains, Drouillard, and Colter were probably the only men who would have recognized that the prints and fire were Shannon's and not some passing Indian's.

I decided to wait for another opportunity and arrived back at the river in time to see three Indian boys jump in the water and swim out to the keelboat. Dorion spoke with them and told the Captain that they were Yankton Sioux boys. The rest of the tribe was a few miles upriver.

"Good," Captain Lewis said. "We'll set up camp here. I want you and Sergeant Pryor to go up there and invite them to parley with us."

That evening the Captain and I went out for a ramble and I picked up Shannon's trail again. I started barking and whimpering and carrying on to get his attention.

"What is it, Sea?"

I ran ahead, with the Captain following close behind. After half a mile I came across a clear moccasin print near some berry bushes where Shannon had been grazing. I barked at the print and the Captain bent down for a closer look.

"No wonder we can't find Shannon," he said. "He's ahead of us! I wonder how far ahead?"

Three days and moving quick, I knew, but I had no way to convey this information.

When we got back to camp, Captain Lewis explained "his" discovery, and the following day he sent Colter out to catch Shannon, loaded with extra provisions, knowing that Shannon would likely have a hollow belly.

Two days later Sergeant Pryor arrived with a group of Yankton Sioux.

"These Yanktons are real friendly," he reported. "They wanted to carry me into their camp on a buffalo hide, but I declined, telling them that I wasn't the chief. When I got there they fed me a fat roasted dog. Delicious!"

I looked around at the men, expecting to see them disgusted by this horror, but all of them just stood there grinning like a bunch of fools. At the time I thought they were just hiding their revulsion.

That night, after Captain Lewis had given his

speech and handed out gifts, the men built three large bonfires and had a party. The Yanktons put on their best buffalo robes and vests decorated with beads, feathers, and porcupine quills. They danced and sang in the firelight to the sound of skin drums and rattles made from deer hooves, which I liked much better than the squeak of the fiddle. The Yankton women danced next, waving around human scalps that had been taken by their fathers and husbands in battles.

Not to be outdone, Private Cruzatte played some whiny tunes on his fiddle and the men danced to the music. One of the French boatmen showed the Yanktons how he could dance on his hands, then York got into the fray, dancing until he nearly collapsed, which impressed the Yanktons greatly. The young girls looked at the ground and covered their shy smiles every time York caught them staring at him in admiration.

The next morning the Yankton chiefs met with the captains before we proceeded on. They told the captains they needed guns, not medals and beads, to protect them from their enemies. The captains said they could not give them guns, but assured them that their new father would give them gifts beyond their imagination if they would go to visit him in Washington. The chiefs said they would go, and Dorion stayed behind to guide them there.

September 6, 1804
Still no sign of our man Shannon... This is truly the
land of plenty. Everywhere we look there are deer, elk,
buffalo, and other creatures previously unknown to me.
But Shannon is no hunter, and I fear he may be
dead....

ONE OF THESE new creatures was a small hoofed animal with stiff, buff-colored hair, large eyes, and short-pronged horns. It was an awkward-looking beast, but it was the fastest thing on hooves I had ever seen. It sped across the ground in long graceful bounds, faster than a bird could fly.

"I swear to god," Colter said, "that animal can out-run a musket ball." It took several days and dozens of shots to prove this theory wrong.

Another animal we discovered during this time was

the whistling rat—at least that's what I thought it was when I first laid eyes on it.

Captain Lewis and I were on a ramble one afternoon when I heard a strange whistling noise in the distance. I ran ahead to see what it was and I came across a whole town of rats. There were thousands of them popping in and out of these holes in the ground, warbling like a flock of songbirds. I tried to catch one to bring back to the Captain, but they dived down their hatches faster than I could snap my jaw closed.

The Captain came along and watched me for a time, then said, "I think we'll need some help with this, Sea. Let's go."

We went back to camp and enlisted a few of the men to help us conquer the rat town.

"Our mission is to capture one alive," the Captain informed them.

A French boatman accompanying us said the animals were not rats, but prairie dogs. He must have been mistaken, because they didn't look or act anything like dogs.

The men tried to dig one out of the ground but gave up after going down six feet without so much as seeing one of the little rat-dogs.

"Any other ideas?" the Captain asked.

"Maybe we could use water to flush them out," Sergeant Gass suggested.

"It's worth a try."

With great difficulty they hauled two barrels of river water up to the rat town and poured the contents down a hole. After a time, one of the soggy animals crawled out into the open and a man grabbed it. We had our live prairie dog. Captain Lewis was delighted with the homely creature. He put it in a box and said he planned to send it back to President Jefferson when the keelboat returned in the spring.

It was a few days after this that we made our best discovery. We came around a sharp bend in the river and Labiche shouted out from the bow, "By god, it's Shannon!"

Sure enough, Private George Shannon was sitting on the bank, grinning from ear to ear despite his pitiful condition. But I don't know who was happier to see whom—the captains and the men nearly wept with joy when they laid eyes on him. He was the youngest of the men and a favorite with everyone.

He said he'd had nothing to eat for the past twelve days but a handful of grapes and a rabbit. "I sat down this morning figuring I was done for. I knew I would never catch up with you, starving like I was. I was just waiting for the Grim Reaper to come along and take me away."

Shannon went on to explain that a few days after he

left us he ran out of balls for his rifle. "I managed to kill the rabbit by whittling down a hunk of wood into a musketball for my gun. Thank god it worked! If it hadn't been for that bit of luck, you'd be burying me right now, boys."

September 24, 1804

I am fearful that our meeting with the Teton Sioux will not go as well as our meeting with the Yanktons. Earlier this afternoon Private Colter informed us that a group of Indians had stolen his horse. A few minutes after we received this information, five young Tetons hailed us from shore, asking if they could ride in the boat. We told them that we would not even talk to any of their people, including the chiefs, until our horse was returned....

I MISSED THE initial meeting with the Teton Sioux because I caught a glimpse of White Feather and had run off into the forest looking for him. When I got back to the men, Captain Lewis had completed his speech and demonstration, and Captain Clark was handing out gifts to the three chiefs. The captains had anchored the keelboat in the middle of the river with men manning the blunderbusses and swivel gun. Along shore were at least two hundred Teton warriors armed with bows and arrows. The air was saturated with the scent of fear and anger. My hackles came to attention.

The three main chiefs—Black Buffalo, the Partisan, and Buffalo Medicine—stared with surly indifference at the gifts they had been given. The Partisan began yowling about his pitiful gift, loud enough for everyone to hear. Buffalo Medicine and Black Buffalo were not about to be outdone by the Partisan, so they started yowling, too.

The captains were dismayed by this turn of events and tried to make it up by inviting all three chiefs out to the keelboat for a tour. When they all got there the captains offered the chiefs a little taste of whiskey, which seemed to settle them down some, but when it was time to take them back to shore in the pirogue the Partisan started stumbling around the deck as if he were drunk, saying that he would not leave.

The captains were furious, but they kept their tempers under control, knowing they could not bodily force the chiefs from the keelboat with a throng of warriors standing alongshore watching their every move. Using several of the men, they were able to gently herd the chiefs back into the pirogue. Captain Lewis stayed aboard the keelboat while Captain Clark and a couple of men quickly rowed the chiefs to shore.

When they got there three of the Partisan's warriors

wrapped themselves around the mast of the pirogue and two other men took hold of the mooring rope. The Partisan said that they would not let the boat go until he was given gifts worthy of his rank. He reckoned that one of our pirogues filled with supplies might do for starters.

Captain Clark's face turned as red as his hair, and he drew his sword from his scabbard.

"Release our pirogue," he shouted. "Now!"

"Prepare arms," Captain Lewis said with icy calmness, lighting a taper and holding it above the keelboat's cannon.

The men on board shouldered their rifles and pointed them toward shore. The Tetons alongshore strung their bows and pointed them at our men.

"On my command," Captain Lewis said quietly. "Not a second before. Steady…"

For a few moments there was complete stillness, as if every living thing were holding its breath. If one of our tribe discharged his musket, or a Teton let an arrow fly— even by accident—the Missouri would flow with blood and our journey would end.

Black Buffalo put an end to the tension by calmly walking over to the warriors holding the rope and telling them to let it go. Reluctantly they obeyed.

"Take the pirogue back to the keelboat," Captain Clark said.

"What about you, Captain?"

"I am not afraid of these Indians and I will not retreat from them, but I don't want them to take our boat. So get it out of here, Private."

As the boat pulled away, Captain Clark was quickly surrounded by Teton warriors. He did not show a hint of fear and began speaking very roughly to them.

As soon as the pirogue got to the keelboat, a dozen men jumped into it and furiously rowed it back to assist Captain Clark. The sight of our men rushing back toward shore with their guns dispersed the crowd.

Captain Clark did not want to leave the situation on a bad note. Before he boarded the pirogue, he approached the chiefs and put his hand out in friendship. Not even Black Buffalo would take his hand, which turned Captain Clark's face red again. He harangued the chiefs with another barrage of choice words no one translated, but the meaning was clear enough. When he'd finished he stomped off toward the pirogue and told the men to shove off.

They hadn't gotten ten feet from shore when Black Buffalo and a couple of his warriors waded out into the water to their waists, begging Captain Clark to take them to the keelboat with him so they might ride in it. Captain Clark softened and picked them up.

As soon as they got to the keelboat the anchors were hauled up and we proceeded a short distance upriver, to an island the captains named Bad Humor. That night no one slept a wink. Even with Black Buffalo as our guest, the men were still fearful the Tetons would attack.

By morning things looked a little brighter. The Partisan joined us and behaved as if nothing had happened the night before. He and Black Buffalo invited the captains up to their villages. The captains stepped away to discuss the invitation.

"Could be a trick," Captain Clark said.

Captain Lewis nodded. "But if it isn't, we don't want to insult them. We still need to do what we can to make peace. I'll take a few men up to the village and see what their intentions are."

Until we saw the village I don't think we knew how lucky we were to have avoided a fight with the Tetons. There were at least eighty tepees spread out over a long distance, housing eight hundred to nine hundred people.

In the center of the village, under guard, were fifty women and children taken prisoner from the Omaha tribe during a recent raid. When Captain Lewis asked about them, Black Buffalo boasted that the Tetons had destroyed forty Omaha lodges and killed seventy-five men and children during the raid.

We wandered around the village for several hours, learning as much as we could about the tribe. The Sioux possessed large herds of horses, which they used for hunting buffalo. They moved the village whenever it suited them, in order to follow the buffalo herds or to find better shelter during the harsh winter. Scattered throughout the village were a number of scrawny dogs, which were made to fend for themselves on whatever bones and scraps of meat they could scrounge from the refuse heap. The Tetons treated their dogs with great contempt, throwing sticks and rocks at them, and kicking them if a foolish cur got within moccasin range. I was glad I was not a Teton dog.

That night there was a big celebration at the village, although there wasn't really anything to celebrate, as there was not a sliver of trust between our two tribes.

Captain Clark asked the chiefs to release the Omaha prisoners. "This gesture would help establish peace with you and the Omahas." The chiefs said they would, but we all knew they had no intention of releasing those poor people.

October 22, 1804
It has been nearly a month since my last entry in this jour-
nal, but this is not because the days have been uneventful. To
the contrary.

We have had a successful council with the Arikara
people—a very friendly tribe. They were astonished by our
airgun. When we offered them a taste of whiskey, they re-
fused, saying they were surprised their great Father to the
east would offer them whiskey, which would make them act
like fools. They gave us bushels of corn, Indian tobacco, and
buffalo robes, which we will need now that winter is upon us.

Several men have joined us on our final push to the
Mandan village, including an Arikara chief who is hopeful
that we can help him achieve peace between his people and
the Mandans....

CAPTAIN LEWIS had not been scratching in the red book
because he was in a serious rambling mood, despite the

prickly pear alongshore. The ground was covered with this spiny cactus and it was hard to find a place to walk without it biting you. On most days we left camp at sunup and walked until after dark. It was as if he knew the coming winter would curtail his rambling and he wanted to get in some extra walking while he still could.

We explored a number of abandoned Indian villages. The Captain went through the empty lodges, looking closely at what was left behind, pacing off how big each village was, and piecing together what it had looked like before the Indians moved on or died from diseases. He wrote this information down in the journal he and Captain Clark were keeping for President Jefferson.

There were thousands of buffalo on the prairie and dozens of wolves hunting them, a fatal dance I never tired of watching. The wolves came to the hunt with a plan in their hearts. They ran at the herd, then watched carefully through the billowing dust for a sign of weakness. When a weak animal was found they cut it out from the herd, running it to exhaustion before moving in for the kill. A wolf snapped at its hind legs, two or three others worried its flanks, and the fastest, strongest wolf latched its teeth onto the buffalo's nose, riding the massive head down until its beard collided with the ground. Sometimes the wolves chose badly. They were gored. They were trampled. They died on the flat dusty prairie. Their steps faltered, but the dance never ended.

Around this time there was another dance going on in our camp. Private Moses Reed was leading it, and the only partner he could find was Private John Newman.

About the only thing Reed had learned from running the gauntlet was not to open his mouth against the captains in the presence of most of the other men. He now transferred his words into Private Newman's head, who in turn spoke them with *his* mouth. Whenever Reed got a chance he would slink up near Newman like a wolf and prey on his mind with poisonous words.

"Do you believe me now? I ran away to get me a better life and now I'm being treated just like a slave—in fact worse than a slave. The captains treat York better than me, better than all of us!

"It's time we did something about this. If we can get a few men on our side before we get to the Mandan village, we can take our oppressors down. Next spring we'll trap a few weeks and go back to our gals with our pouches filled with money.

"We won't get that land they promised us, I can tell you that. Those Tetons almost killed the lot of us and some of the Indians up ahead are worse. We're going to die out here. Every last one of us, we're all going to die.

And that girl of yours back home? How long do you think she's going to wait around for you?"

Hearing these words day after day was just too much for poor Newman. One night the men sat around the fire talking about this and that—the Arikara women, what the Mandan women would be like, would it ever stop raining, how cold the winter would be....

Newman was sitting quietly, as he usually did, staring into the fire, holding a cup of hot coffee in his hands to warm them—when suddenly he stood up and threw his mug onto the ground.

"I'm sick of being a slave!" he shouted. "Aren't all of you? It's time we knock the captains down a peg or two and take this expedition over! Who's with me?"

The men stared at him in mute bewilderment. Not even John Colter, who was seldom wordless, had anything to say.

"You're all cowards!" Newman spit. "I'm a young man with my whole life before me, and I intend to live it as a free man!"

Captain Clark, having heard the commotion all the way from the keelboat, strolled up to the fire. "Private Newman, would you care to recant those mutinous words you have spoken?"

Private Newman glared at him defiantly. "No sir, I would not."

"Confine him," Captain Clark said calmly, and strolled back to the keelboat.

The next day a court-martial was held and Newman was charged with expressing mutinous words. He was sentenced to seventy-five lashes, removal from the permanent party, and hard labor until he could be sent back to Saint Louis in the spring with the French boatmen.

After the lashing Newman was a changed man. He recanted what he had said and stopped listening to Reed. He hoped he could get back into the captains' good graces and continue with us in the spring, but the captains could not afford to have a weak-spirited or mutinous man as a member of the permanent party.

October 26, 1804

Tomorrow morning I will walk ahead to the Mandan village and make certain of our welcome.

I spent a good portion of the morning looking over my animal collection, in particular the prairie wolf Captain Clark managed to kill a few weeks ago. The animal is quite different from the larger gray wolf and is definitely a different species, but certainly a canine of some type. It was a female....

IT WAS MY LITTLE beauty, whom I had not seen since the captains had fired upon her and missed. I knew she was still following us, but she seemed to have grown cautious again after her brush with the captains. I had hoped that experience would prevent her from showing herself again. It did not.

Captain Clark shot her while I was on a ramble with Captain Lewis. When we got back to camp we found her stiffened body lying on the keelboat deck, her golden eyes dulled by death. I could not watch as the Captain measured her and stripped her fur away.

Colter yawns.

"How much more is there?" Drouillard asks.

"A good bit more," Colter says, flipping through the pages.

Drouillard looks at Mountain Dog and Watkuweis. "Colter's eyes are getting sore. We will continue reading tomorrow."

Watkuweis takes the red book, slips it back into the otter skin pouch, and hands it to Mountain Dog. "We will return tomorrow night," she says.

Colter and Drouillard watch them walk away and spread their blankets on the ground.

"So where the devil do you think they got that book?" Colter asks.

"Guess we'll find out after you finish reading it," Drouillard says.

Within a few minutes both men are asleep.

EARLY THE NEXT morning I follow Mountain Dog out onto the prairie to help search for buffalo. It takes us all day to find a herd, and we don't get back to camp until after dark.

After we eat, Mountain Dog gets the otter bag from his tepee and we join Drouillard and Colter at their fire.

"Are Colter's eyes rested?" Watkuweis asks Drouillard.

"I suspect so," he says with a smile. "He's had them closed most of the day."

"What did she say?" Colter asks.

"She wants you to read."

Colter opens the red book....

October 29, 1804
We are now with the Mandans, trying to find a good spot to
build our winter fort.
    There was a prairie fire this morning in which several
Mandans were burned to death while they were out hunting
buffalo....

WHEN THE INFERNO died down, I followed Drouillard
and Tabeau out onto the scorched flatland to view the
devastation. We found the charred remains of buffalo,
wolves, foxes, rabbits, and humans.

"Gray Squirrel and his wife, Running Water,"
Tabeau said, looking down at two bodies. "Grass fires
move as fast as the wind. They didn't have a chance."

"Caw! Caw! Caw!"

White Feather landed on a burnt buffalo skin not
far from the bodies. It had been a long time since I had

seen him, and I figured he had stopped following us. I was happy he was back.

"Caw! Caw! Caw!"

Drouillard and Tabeau continued their conversation and did not give the crow a single glance. I walked over to the buffalo skin and White Feather flew away. Something moved beneath the skin and I started digging. There was a cry to go along with a movement, which quickly turned into a loud wailing. Drouillard pushed me aside and Tabeau flipped the skin over. It was a child making the noise.

"I'll be," Tabeau said. "Gray Squirrel's son. When the fire came they must have rolled him up in the wet skin. There isn't a blister on him."

"Why didn't they crawl under the skin themselves?"

"Not big enough."

Drouillard picked the boy up and carried him back to the Mandan village.

November 3, 1804
We have started building our fort. It is located across from
the first Mandan village....

THERE WERE TWO Mandan villages, one on the east side
of the Missouri and one on the west side. A little farther north were three Hidatsa villages situated on the
smaller Knife River.

The Mandans lived in large earth lodges about forty
feet around. In each village there were forty lodges, with
at least ten people living in each lodge. At night they
brought their horses and dogs right into the lodge to
sleep alongside them.

The men built our fort across from the first Mandan
village. The gated wall surrounding the fort was made
out of stout trees and stood eighteen feet tall. The captains had the swivel gun put on top of the wall in case
we were attacked. Inside were two rows of small huts for

the men to sleep in, a foundry, and a plaza to hold council with the Indians, of whom there was a steady flow.

The Mandan and Hidatsa villages functioned like the wharves I had grown up on, but instead of using money, transactions were based purely on trade. Each lodge was a store filled with goods. Cheyenne, Arikara, Sioux, Otos, French and English from Canada, Spaniards, and men and women from half a dozen other tribes traveled across the prairie sea to trade their wares here. A good horse might cost three tanned buffalo robes, one hundred blue beads, and twenty pounds of corn. The Indian who traded the horse would take what he got and trade it for something he and his family needed.

The Mandans were experienced traders. When we first arrived they offered us a few gifts of meat and corn, but after that it was all business. Dozens of Mandans showed up at the fort every day with bushels of corn and squash, meat, buffalo robes, furs, and other items. The men would sit down with them in the plaza and the long process of haggling over prices would begin.

It wasn't long before the cold descended and held us in its icy fist. The river froze solid and our men walked around with buffalo robes wrapped around themselves, the hair sides against their bodies. The Mandans didn't seem to be bothered by the cold. They wore thin moccasins and often spent the night out on the windswept prairie without a fire or a robe to keep them warm. Because of my fur, I was not particularly bothered by the cold. In fact I preferred the cold to the heat of summer.

When the men were off duty they huddled around the fires in their huts, trying to keep the chill away, or walked over to the Mandan villages to visit with the women.

The captains spent most of their time inside the fort. Captain Lewis worked on his notes for President Jefferson, and Captain Clark refined the maps of where we had been.

One day a Frenchman named Toussaint Charbonneau showed up at the fort and walked in on Captain Lewis unannounced, catching him in the middle of working on his animal collection. Charbonneau did not know better than to disturb the Captain when he was working.

"My name is Toussaint Charbonneau," he said with a heavy accent. "I would like to be your interpreter."

Captain Lewis looked up and glared at the intruder for a full minute without uttering one word. Charbonneau had a bushy unkempt beard, shoulder-length gray hair, and a unique smell to him that I placed somewhere between a buffalo's and a raccoon's. He took his hat off. The top of his head was as bald as a newborn mouse pup. While the Captain continued his silent stare, Charbonneau looked around the hut casually, without the slightest idea that his host was irritated.

"We already have an interpreter," Captain Lewis said finally, and looked back down at the skull he had been examining.

"You mean Drouillard?"

Captain Lewis looked up again as if he were surprised that Charbonneau was still standing there. "That's exactly who I mean."

"Ha!" Charbonneau slapped his ample belly.

Captain Lewis flushed in anger. He didn't like this loud Frenchman and he was about to throw him out of the hut when Captain Clark walked in.

Captain Lewis took a deep breath to calm himself. "We have a visitor," he said. "This is Toussaint Charbonneau."

"I've heard the name," Captain Clark said, putting his hand out. "You live up with the Hidatsas?"

"Yes, I do."

"He wants to be our interpreter," Captain Lewis said.

"But we have an—"

"I have already told Mr. Charbonneau that George Drouillard is our interpreter. He was not impressed."

"Perhaps I should start again," Charbonneau offered, finally seeing the Captain's annoyance.

"By all means," Captain Lewis said.

"I didn't mean any offense. I'm sure your man Drouillard is a good man, but does he speak fluent Shoshone?"

The captains looked at each other in surprise, not sure they understood. None of us had ever even seen a Shoshone Indian. But the captains were depending on the Shoshone tribe to sell us horses when we reached the mountains next summer. Making peace with the Shoshones and trading for their horses would be critical to the success of the expedition. The captains had been talking about the problem just that morning over breakfast.

"And I suppose you speak fluent Shoshone?" Captain Lewis asked.

Charbonneau launched into an involved answer, but Captain Lewis didn't understand what he was saying. "Tabeau!" he called. Tabeau stuck his head into the hut. "Can you find out if this man actually speaks the Shoshone language?"

Charbonneau and Tabeau spoke in French for several minutes.

"He does not speak Shoshone," Tabeau explained. "But he has two Shoshone wives living with him up at the Hidatsa village. The women were captured in a Hidatsa raid a few years ago and Charbonneau here won them in a bet with the warriors who owned them. He says he'll bring them with him. He also says that he's a skilled boatman."

The captains asked Tabeau to take Charbonneau outside.

"What do you think?" Captain Lewis asked.

"We need someone who can speak Shoshone. I don't suppose he'll allow one of his wives to come along without him."

"Probably not. And even if he were willing, having an unescorted woman along could pose a problem."

Captain Clark nodded in agreement. "We could use another boatman."

"True."

The captains talked for quite some time before calling Charbonneau back in. After another long discussion they reached an agreement with him. Charbonneau would be hired, and he would bring one of his wives with him.

The following week he brought his two wives to the fort. They were just girls, no more than fifteen or sixteen years old. When they were introduced to the captains they stared down at the ground shyly. Charbonneau had chosen the girl named Sacagawea to accompany us in the spring. "In the Hidatsa language," he said, "Sacagawea means Bird Woman."

The name fit her well. She was a small-boned girl with long crow-colored hair, pulled back and braided in the Indian way. I walked up to her and she immediately scratched my ears. As I stood there enjoying her attentions, I picked up an odd scent from her that could mean only one thing—Bird Woman was carrying a pup inside her. The captains were clearly unaware of this, and I suspected Charbonneau was no less ignorant. They would all find out soon enough.

When they left, Captain Lewis said, "I hope Sacagawea is strong enough to endure the rigors of our journey."

Bird Woman would surprise us all.

January 12, 1805
We brought in the New Year by taking a large group of men
to the first Mandan village for dancing and merriment. A
good time was had by all....

WE ENJOYED our time among the Mandans, but after a
few weeks the men were already talking about proceeding on, hoping for an early spring. I was eager to leave
as well. I had gotten used to wandering and discovering
new sights and smells. The fort was secure and comfortable, but also confining. I spent a good part of each
day roaming through the Mandan villages or out hunting with Droulliard.

Captain Lewis spent most days inside the fort, working on his notes and preparing his collection, which
would be sent back with the French voyagers in the
spring.

As the winter progressed, food became scarce. Our hunters often came back hungry and frostbitten, without a scrap of meat to show for their efforts.

The captains started doctoring the Indians in exchange for meat and produce. They treated wounds, colds, rheumatism, bad teeth, frostbite, and a number of other ailments. The word spread and every morning a dozen Indians lined up outside the captains' huts, each with an armful of food, to wait their turn for the white medicine.

A second business was set up using the forge and the blacksmith and gunsmith skills of Private John Shields. The Indians brought in hoes that needed mending, axes that needed sharpening, and broken rifles. Eventually there wasn't a broken hoe in any of the Mandan and Hidatsa lodges. The axes were all sharpened, and all the Indians' rifles were as good as new.

Business dropped off. The captains remedied this by helping Shields design a battle-ax—an item that became so popular he and the men helping him could hardly keep up with the demand.

I thought Shield's ax business was a little odd. On the one hand, the captains were telling the Indians to stop warring with one another. On the other hand, they were making battle-axes that the Indians would certainly use in raids. One day a Hidatsa war chief stopped by the Captain's hut on his way to pick up a battle-ax at the forge. He asked permission to raid the Sioux and Arikaras when the weather broke in spring. He got the ax but was told not to use it, which I could see made no sense to him.

February 11, 1805
Sacagawea began her labor today. Captain Clark and I are
tending her, but the birth is taking an inordinate amount of
time. I have grown very fond of her since she and her hus-
band moved into the fort with us....

THE CAPTAIN wasn't alone in his feelings for Bird
Woman. Soon after she and Charbonneau moved into
the fort, she announced that she was pregnant. There
was some heated debate among the men over the wisdom of her joining our tribe. They thought a woman
with a child would be too much of a burden. But as they
got to know her, the subject began to fade. There was
something about her quiet shyness that appealed to all
the men. And by the time she gave birth, they were
looking forward to having a human pup on the journey.

Bird Woman spent many evenings picking burrs out
of my fur. And from time to time she slipped me a dead

mouse, because she knew I was partial to them. These two acts of kindness were more than enough to endear her to me forever.

Bird Woman's labor was long. The captains fretted over her as if *they* were the expectant fathers, not Charbonneau. After a time René Jessaume, one of the French traders living with the Mandans, suggested to Captain Lewis that he feed her a bit of rattlesnake rattle to hurry the labor along. "It works every time," René insisted.

Captain Lewis was doubtful, but he was getting desperate. He broke up a bit of rattlesnake rattle, put it into a cup of water, and offered it to her.

Sure enough, a few minutes after she drank the mixture down, our tribe had a new member. They named the pup Jean Baptiste Charbonneau, but Captain Clark called him Pomp, which is the name that seemed to stick.

About a month after Pomp was born Charbonneau and his family got kicked out of the fort. The problem began when the captains sat down with Charbonneau to go over his contract and he became uppity with them. He told the captains he would not perform any camp duties, carry any loads, or stand guard duty. He also informed them that he expected to be free to leave the party at any time and that they would have to supply him with provisions if he did. This of course was unacceptable and he was asked to leave that very day.

The captains were very disappointed at this turn of events and so were the men. The fort just wasn't the same without Bird Woman and Pomp. The men missed making faces and uttering odd guttural sounds at her pup. I missed them, too.

A few days after their departure I crossed the frozen river to the Mandan village where they were staying, to see how they were doing in their new circumstances.

Long before I reached the village I heard Bird Woman's voice, but she sounded more like an angry bear than a bird. She was calling her husband every bad name she could think of in Shoshone and Hidatsa. As best I could figure out between curses, Bird Woman wanted to go home to her family below the big mountains and could not believe Charbonneau's arrogance had ruined this prospect.

I did not hear Charbonneau utter a single word all during this harangue. The conversation was so one-sided, I thought she must have killed him and she was shouting at his corpse; but I was wrong. The buffalo-hide door of the lodge flew open and he stumbled outside in a daze, with Bird Woman still shouting at him.

Charbonneau found Tabeau and begged him to go over to the fort and intercede with the captains on his behalf. He told Tabeau that he would do anything the captains asked if they would just allow him and Bird Woman to go with them.

Tabeau crossed over to the fort and argued the case. The captains let Charbonneau stew for a few more days in Bird Woman's wrath, but they finally gave in and hired him back.

March 30, 1805

Our preparations for departure are nearly complete and within a week we will be on our way. Captain Clark and I have written a detailed letter to President Jefferson outlining our journey thus far. We will also be sending back the animal and plant collection and some of our notes.

From this point on we will be traveling into uncharted territory, but I am confident we will discover the Northwest Passage if what the Hidatsas have told us is true. We will be traveling in our two pirogues and in six dugout canoes the men have made, all of which have been rigged with sails. With these smaller boats we should make 25 miles a day, arriving at the Pacific this summer and perhaps even returning to Fort Mandan before winter.

Captain Clark and I are confident in the 26 men we have chosen to continue on with us in the permanent party. We have organized the privates into three squads, with a sergeant over each squad. In addition we travel with five

civilians—York, Drouillard, Charbonneau, Sacagawea, and
Pomp.

*   I am so eager to leave, I can barely sleep at night....*

OUR FINAL DAYS at Fort Mandan were hectic, but at last
the men were ready and the boats were loaded. The
keelboat headed back down the Missouri toward Saint
Louis with the French voyagers and the men not as-
signed to the permanent party. On board were all of the
captains' notes, the dead animal collection, four live
magpies, a live prairie dog, a live prairie hen, and
Privates Reed and Newman.

After the long winter Captain Lewis wanted to
stretch his legs and decided to walk alongshore. I led
the way. We proceeded on.

The men tired easily at first. The long winter at Fort
Mandan had softened them and the lack of meat had
not helped matters. The Indians seemed to have killed
nearly every animal for a hundred miles, and the few
our hunters managed to shoot were in poor flesh after
the harsh winter.

On most days I stayed on shore foraging, unless the
Captain made me ride in the boat, which he seldom
did. Sometimes I rambled by myself, sometimes with
the Captain, sometimes with the hunters, and sometimes with Bird Woman.

She walked with little Pomp strapped to her back on a cradleboard, bundled in blankets and skins, with only his little black eyes and nose exposed. On warm days his arms were freed to play with his mother's black hair as she walked with her head down, looking for plants and roots and mice nests, which she found faster than I could smell them. When she discovered a nest, she opened it with a stick to retrieve the hog peanuts the mice had stored.

I was more interested in the mice than the peanuts, but the rodents were so quick I was lucky to catch one out of every other nest. And Bird Woman didn't allow me to eat the pink baby mice. The first time I tried to snap one of the blind squirmers up, she whacked me a good one across the nose with her stick. "Bad dog! It is wrong to eat babies that cannot run away."

She always left a couple of peanuts in the nest for the mice to eat, and covered the babies before she proceeded on.

At night the captains slept in a buffaloskin lodge along with Drouillard, Charbonneau, Sacagawea, and Pomp. I slept nearest to the door, so I could get out quickly if I heard something outside.

Charbonneau snored louder than any man I have ever heard, which added to Captain Lewis's irritation with him.

Before we left Fort Mandan Charbonneau had assured the captains he was a skilled boatman, but it became clear that this was not true. I was in his boat one day with Captain Lewis, Sacagawea, Pomp, Drouillard, and three men who could not swim. A sudden squall came up, turning the boat sideways. Charbonneau sat at the tiller frozen in fear, despite Captain Lewis's shouting at him to swing the bow into the current. The boat nearly sank with all of our trade goods, to say nothing of the men who could not swim. Drouillard, ever steady in the face of disaster, calmly lowered the sail and the boat righted itself. If it were not for Sacagawea, I am sure the captains would have sent Charbonneau back to the Mandan village that afternoon.

About this time an Indian dog showed up in camp. I had smelled it following us for several days and hoped it had the sense not to show itself, but its hunger drove it into camp late one evening. It slunk into the firelight and flopped down right in front of me. Poor thing. Bones sticking out, open sores on the skin.

"Look, Seaman has a girlfriend!"

"He could do better than that."

"Followed him all the way from the Mandan village."

She was not a Mandan or Hidatsa dog. She had been out on her own for quite some time.

Drouillard threw her a scrap of beaver meat, but she didn't touch it, fearing I might attack her. I backed away to give her room and she snapped up the meat and bolted back into the trees. Now that she had gotten a taste of food I knew she would be back, and I hoped she wouldn't suffer the same fate as my prairie wolf.

I had not seen White Feather since the fire on the Mandan prairie. Every time I heard a crow I would run to the sound and was disappointed when I found the cawing came from a common crow.

April 20, 1805

We have been held in camp for several days due to severe winds and I've taken advantage of our stay by making a thorough exploration of this area. I found a dead Indian on a scaffold not far from our camp. Lying next to him were several baskets, his tomahawk, the body of his dog, and his sled. The Indians often sacrifice the animals that have helped them in life. I explained to Sea that I didn't think this would be necessary in his case if I should pass on, and for a moment I thought he understood what I was talking about.

We have traveled far enough upriver from the Mandan and Hidatsa villages to see the game increase, which is a great relief to all of us. There are a number of dead buffalo along this stretch of river, caught on snags or washed up on shore. They must have fallen through the ice and drowned. Wolves and other animals feast on their soft flesh, and near one of the carcasses we

saw bear tracks bigger than anything I could have
imagined....

"MUST BE ONE OF those grizzly bears," Captain Clark said. "Look at the size of that track."

We had heard about grizzly bears from the Mandan villagers. The Mandans also called them white bears because when such a bear gets older the tips of its hairs turn lighter. The Indians and the French trappers were scared of them, and it was no wonder. The tracks were huge. Not only this, the bear had dragged that buffalo a good fifteen feet farther up the bank in the soft sand. The idea of an animal that could leave a print that deep and move a buffalo that far made the hair on my back stand straight up. I knew right then that I would not like grizzly bears.

"I don't blame the Indians for being afraid of them," Captain Lewis said. "I wouldn't want to face a bear that size with a bow and arrow. But we will have no trouble with our rifles."

It was whelping time on the prairie. The next morning Captain Clark shot a buffalo. As York gutted and skinned it we watched a pack of wolves pull down a calf that could not keep up with the herd. The calf's mother came back and tried to defend her pup. She stamped her feet and lowered her head to charge, but this did not frighten the wolves. In fact, the lead wolf jumped right onto her back. She shook him off, but fear had gotten the better of her and she galloped away and joined the herd without her calf.

That same afternoon, while Captain Lewis and I were returning to camp, a buffalo calf followed us. It wasn't much bigger than I am. I think it would have followed us all the way back to camp, but Captain Lewis started laughing and the sound scared the calf away.

"I believe he thought you were a buffalo calf, Sea," Captain Lewis said. "You're about the right size and shape. Better watch yourself, or one of our men will shoot you."

April 24, 1805
Once again we are stranded in camp because of severe wind.
Tomorrow, weather permitting, the boats will proceed on,
but regardless of the wind, I plan to lead a few men ahead in
search of the Yellowstone River, which should be less than a
day's march....

THAT NIGHT the temperature fell and the wind stopped
as if it were frozen in place. At sunrise, when the
boats started upriver, it was so cold the water froze to
the oars.

The men in our shore party were grateful to be afoot
rather than paddling on the cold river. As we rambled
we saw hundreds of buffalo and elk who showed virtually no fear of us, even though we passed within yards of
them.

"They don't even run, Captain."

"We could kill them with clubs."

"I suspect they haven't seen too many humans," the Captain replied. "They'll learn."

That evening we reached the Yellowstone River. Drouillard shot a buffalo not a hundred feet from our camp. The herd scattered at the sound of his gun. They were learning.

The next day the boats caught up to us. In the evening the captains handed around a dram of whiskey and Cruzatte brought out his fiddle.

I didn't participate in the festivities. Instead I went for a ramble with the Indian dog, who shared my opinion of fiddle music. The cold night was clear and well lit by a full moon. We followed the Yellowstone River for several miles, stopping once in a while to check a smell or mark a bush. The buffalo grazed and grunted on the open plain. Elk and deer were everywhere. Wolves howled, which quickened our blood.

Sometimes I led the way, then I would drop back and let the Indian dog lead. We came to a high bank above the river. The Indian dog stopped and looked down.

Below us a small herd of antelope were swimming across the river. On the other side was a pack of wolves. When the antelope saw the wolves, they allowed the current to take them farther downriver so they wouldn't come ashore where the wolves were waiting. The wolves were not fooled. They simply followed along on shore, knowing the antelope could not stay in the water forever. Eventually the first antelope stumbled into the shallows and was taken before it left the water. Another was taken farther down. The rest escaped because the pack had what it needed.

I wasn't hungry, but my blood was tingling. I wanted to join in the hunt. I turned to find a path to the river, but to my horror my way was blocked by a grizzly.

It reared up on its hind legs, blotting the moon out with its gigantic head, then bellowed with a ferociousness that turned my legs to hot tallow. For a moment I could not move. How could I have let a gigantic bear sneak up on me? I looked for the Indian dog and caught a glimpse of her tail disappearing over the edge of the cliff. The bear stopped bellowing, and I heard the Indian dog splash into the river below.

The bear came down heavily on his front feet and rushed me. I had only one chance. Just before I jumped I felt the bear's warm breath on my neck. I turned my head as I fell, expecting to see him falling behind me, but instead he was standing on the edge, bellowing in rage.

I hit the ice-cold water and the current dragged me under. When I resurfaced I was a long way from the bear. I swam to the opposite shore, climbed out, and shook the water out of my fur.

There was a sudden movement to my left, but before I could turn to face it, something rushed from the bushes to my right. Wolves! Four of them. They circled around me cautiously, not sure how much strength I had—it wasn't much after my long swim. One came in from behind. I caught his ear near the base and he yelped as he tore the ear from my grip. But it was only a matter of time before they wore me down. Once again my only hope was the river. Wolves are not fond of water and with so much game around I doubted they would pursue me. I rushed the wolf closest to the river. She crouched with her jaws open to meet my charge, but I jumped right over her and into the water, letting the current take me.

The water was cold and swift—sadly, too cold and too swift for the Indian dog. I washed right past her body, which was caught on a snag, and felt deep sadness that the dance was now over for her.

The wolves ran alongshore, following my progress, but they gave up just as the sun began to rise. I climbed out of the river and followed the shoreline back to our camp.

The men were already up, eating breakfast. Captain Lewis was scratching in the red book while York and Bird Woman fried meat and boiled coffee on his fire.

The Captain looked up from the book. "There you are, Sea! I wondered where you had gone off to. Out for an early morning swim?"

A few days later I got my chance to take my first antelope. The men were loading the dugouts. Drouillard and I saw the antelope crossing the river at the same moment. Drouillard reached for his powder horn, but before he could charge his rifle I was in the water and had the antelope in my mouth. I pulled it under the water and held it there until it stopped struggling, then I dragged it up on shore.

"The dog saved you a ball, Drouillard."

"With a dog like that we don't need guns."

"We have our own wolf!"

April 29, 1805
This afternoon I shot a grizzly bear. I think this bear's feroc-
ity is greatly exaggerated....

Colter laughs. "We changed our minds pretty darn
quick about that."
Drouillard nods.

CAPTAIN LEWIS, Drouillard, and I were walking through
a thick stand of trees about a mile in from the river. The
wind changed direction suddenly, sending the unmistakable scent of grizzly bear to my nose. I started barking.
"Quiet!" Captain Lewis hushed me.
With difficulty I obeyed. He had no idea then what
lay in the clearing on the other side of the trees, but he
found out soon enough.
"Bears," Drouillard said, pointing.

Two of them, not a hundred paces away. One of the grizzlies stood up on its hind feet and put its nose in the air, trying to figure out what we were. The other bear turned and ran. Drouillard fired at the running bear. Captain Lewis took the standing bear. Drouillard's shot hit home, but the bear didn't even break stride. The Captain's shot hit the standing bear square in the chest. It plopped down on its front feet and charged us.

"Run!" Captain Lewis shouted.

I was halfway back to the river before I realized that Captain Lewis and Drouillard were not with me. I stopped and sniffed the air to see if I could pick up what had happened, but it didn't tell me anything. I proceeded back to the clearing cautiously, not knowing what I would see, and hoping it wouldn't be the grizzly feasting on their mauled corpses. When I broke through the trees I was relieved to see Captain Lewis and Drouillard both on their feet, standing over a dead grizzly. The bear had fallen from his chest wound before he reached the woods.

Captain Lewis was examining the bear's teeth and claws. "Not as formidable as the legend," he commented.

That bear was about one-third the size of the bear I'd encountered along the river.

May 14, 1805

We are making good progress, but as each day passes I am increasingly worried about reaching the Rocky Mountains before the bad weather sets in.

I have started saving elk skins for the iron boat I designed. Although the men have grumbled about carrying the heavy frame all these months, they will be glad once they see how well it works. I look forward to the day we put it together.

I have changed my opinion of grizzly bears. Last week it took ten well-placed balls to kill one of these bears—a truly monstrous beast! And three days ago Private Bratton came into camp saying he had shot a grizzly but was not able to kill it. The bear chased him a considerable distance and it would have caught him if it hadn't been severely wounded. I sent seven men out to kill this bear, and after two shots through the skull the bear finally died. It had covered a distance of over a mile after Bratton had shot it through the lungs. I think I would rather fight two Indians with my bare hands than one of these bears.

I have ordered the men walking alongshore to do so in twos and threes to better protect them from these beasts, but had I seen a grizzly this evening I would readily have fed Charbonneau to it. He is the most incompetent boatman I have ever seen and today he very nearly lost our most precious possessions....

WHEN THE TROUBLE began the captains were both on shore watching the men paddle the boats upriver. The wind filled the sails, but it was still a hard pull against the fast current. Suddenly a squall came up, turning the white pirogue sideways. The pirogue heeled over and began to fill with water.

"Turn into the current!" Captain Lewis shouted. "Turn into the current!"

The men aboard could not hear him above the sound of the water and their own shouting. Both captains fired their rifles, trying to get the crew's attention, which had no effect. Charbonneau, who was manning the rudder, let go, looked up at the sky, and yelled, "Dear god, have mercy on my soul!"

"Our journals!" Captain Lewis shouted. "Our maps!" He dropped his rifle and began stripping.

The current was too treacherous even for me, and I

was a better swimmer than all the men put together. I barked at him, but he paid no attention. Captain Clark saw the danger, too. He threw his arms around Captain Lewis and shouted, "No, Meriwether!"

"But our supplies!"

"They're useless if you drown."

"We'll lose everything!" Captain Lewis said helplessly.

Just then Cruzatte, who was in the bow of the boat, pointed his rifle at Charbonneau and shouted, "If you don't grab that rudder and swing us back into the current, I'll blow your blame head off!"

Charbonneau, more frightened of a musket ball than of drowning, retook the rudder, and the bow swung back into the current. But by this time the boat was filled with water to the top of the gunwale, looking a great deal like a floating bathtub.

After several minutes of frantic bailing, the crew managed to paddle the leaden boat to shore, where all but Charbonneau jumped out and helped the captains secure the bow before the current caught it again.

All during this disaster Bird Woman was as calm as could be. With Pomp strapped on her back, she had gathered every paper and box within reach, saving a great many items from being swept away in the current.

"Unload the supplies," Captain Lewis said. "We'll camp here until everything has dried." He looked at the only remaining passenger through narrowed eyes. "Charbonneau, I'd like a word with you."

Charbonneau, still holding the rudder, did not budge. Captain Lewis ignored him for the moment and began taking his instruments out of their cases and drying them. Eventually Charbonneau gathered enough courage to wade across the boat to shore. Bird Woman had a wry smile on her face as she spread the papers she had saved on the ground and weighted them with rocks.

"Looks like we'll be getting *boudin blanc* for the next few days," Private Shannon said.

Every time Charbonneau got in trouble he made his specialty, *boudin blanc,* or buffalo sausage—Captain Lewis's favorite dish. After a few plates of sausage the Captain always seemed to forget what inspired Charbonneau to make it in the first place.

"Come with me, Mister Charbonneau," Captain Lewis said.

Charbonneau hung his gray head and followed.

That same afternoon I picked up a scent I hadn't smelled since I was with Brady. It brought back happy memories of grand chases with few consequences.

At every dock along the Ohio River there were fish, and where there were fish, there were nimble cats. I didn't expect to find a cat out here, but the scent was unmistakable. I followed it for a couple miles to a cave above the river. The space was too narrow for me to squeeze through, but I didn't let this stop my fun. I stuck my head inside the cave and barked as loudly as I could.

Something rushed me from the dark cavern, hissing like no cat I'd ever heard before. I backed away, and a cat nearly as large as I was burst through the opening with such force it over jumped me by fifteen feet. She turned around in midair and landed, facing me in a crouch. Her eyes were fiery yellow, her fur was the color of antelope, and her snarling teeth were sharp. But what had me most worried were her unsheathed claws. I had been swiped a time or two on the nose, but these daggers were big enough to turn me into a pile of Charbonneau's *boudin blanc*. Cats were not supposed to come in this size! It just wasn't natural.

I thought once again of the river, knowing that cats do not like the water any more than wolves do. Unfortunately the enormous cat was in my way. Her thick, black-tipped tail lashed back and forth as if it were tied to a string from the sky.

Just then a rifle discharged below us with a loud bang. The cat jumped at the sound and I launched myself past her, landing on my chin and rolling all the way to the bottom of the hill, where I stopped at Colter's feet.

"What is it?" Colter looked around in terror, recharging his rifle as fast as I've ever seen a man do it.

"Grizzly?" He swung the rifle in the direction of the hill.

The cat was not there.

"Sea, you've got to stop surprising people like that," Colter said, relaxing a little. "It's not funny. You'll get your head blown off."

He walked over to the deer he had shot and quickly gutted it. I stared up the hillside, shivering like an Indian rattle.

"Aren't you hungry, boy?"

I was, but I didn't even look at the pile of guts. My full attention was on the hill.

"Suit yourself," Colter said, hefting the deer over his shoulder. "I'm heading back to camp before the others get all the *boudin blanc*."

I stuck to Colter like hot tree pitch, glancing behind me all the way back to camp.

May 19, 1805
Two nights ago the tree directly above our lodge caught fire.
If it hadn't been for my dog warning us, everyone inside
would have perished. As soon as we crawled out, fiery
branches fell on top of our shelter and collapsed it.

And today I am afraid my fine dog might die. One of
the men wounded a beaver and Sea jumped into the water to
retrieve it. The beaver bit him on the leg, severing an artery,
and he has lost a great deal of blood. I have stemmed the
flow, but he is doing poorly. I fear his luck has run out....

GRIZZLIES, WOLVES, the enormous cat—but it was a beaver that nearly did me in.

Cruzatte shot the beaver from the bow of the pirogue, and not having the best eyesight of the men, he only wounded it. I was onshore at the time and, fearing that the beaver was going to escape, I jumped in the water after it. The beaver's hind leg was broken and I easily overtook it, but as I was about to take hold, the beaver dived and took hold of me! It bit my leg deep with its razor-sharp teeth and the water turned pink with my blood. By the time I got to shore my strength was gone and I couldn't get to my feet.

Captain Lewis directed the pirogue to shore and was out of the boat twenty feet before it landed, splashing his way to where I lay.

"Get the medical kit!"

The next thing I remember I was in the lodge. It was dark, except for a single flickering candle. My head was in the Captain's lap. He was sound asleep, with his hand resting on my head and the red book open on the blanket covering me. My leg was wrapped up tight and it hurt terribly.

The next morning the Captain would not allow me to stand up. He carried me to the pirogue wrapped in that blanket and told the men to take it easy on the water so I didn't get bumped around—a command impossible to obey.

For the next few days I rode in the boat and the Captain wouldn't let me put any weight on my sore leg. My luck had not run out, though. I recovered well and it wasn't long before I had so much energy built up I could not stay still. When the men weren't looking I jumped into the river, swam to shore, and found

Captain Lewis. I thought he might be cross when he saw me, but instead he laughed.

"So you gave them the slip?" He scratched my head. "I thought you might when you felt up to it."

The leg healed, but it has never been quite the same since.

May 26, 1805
Today I beheld the Rocky Mountains for the first time. I could see only a few of the snow-covered peaks above the horizon, but with the sun reflecting off them they were a wonderful sight to see. I could hardly contain my pleasure, knowing that we are now nearly at the end of the Missouri River, but this pleasure in seeing the mountains is somewhat confounded by my fear of crossing them. I know it is a crime to anticipate evil, so I am trying to imagine an easy passage through those peaks....

THE MOUNTAINS were whiter and taller than any of us could have imagined, and Captain Lewis stared at them until sunset. He was right to worry about getting through them, but before we reached the mountains we would face a number of other dangers. Like the lone buffalo who stampeded our camp one night.

Since my injury I had been sleeping toward the back

of the lodge, next to Captain Lewis, where it was warmer. Because of this I didn't hear the buffalo swim across the river, clamber over the white pirogue, smash York's rifle, and damage the blunderbusses.

What I did hear was *Caw! Caw! Caw!* My eyes snapped open at the familiar call, then I heard Charbonneau, who had sentry duty that night, shout. I was up in an instant, scrambling past the captains, Drouillard, Bird Woman, and Pomp. By the time I got through the flap the buffalo was charging right through the middle of camp.

The big brute ran straight for our lodge, where the Captain and the others were still stumbling around inside. I ran at the buffalo head-on, as I'd seen the wolves do on many occasions. Just as we were about to collide I stepped to the side and bit into the buffalo's ear. The beast veered to the left, missing the lodge by five feet, and I went for a wild ride until I remembered to unclench my jaws. When I stopped somersaulting over the rough ground and looked up, the buffalo was gone.

"His hoof didn't land a foot from my durn head!"

"I thought it was a grizzly!"

"Lucky some of us weren't killed!"

"The dog saved the captains' lives!"

"I saw him! He went right for that bull!"

"Hung on to him like a prickly pear!"

The captains walked down to the white pirogue with torches to survey the damage. Everyone followed.

"Who was on sentry duty?" Captain Lewis asked.

This quieted everyone down. The men looked at Charbonneau.

"You didn't hear the buffalo coming over the top of the pirogue?" Captain Lewis asked.

"No, I did not."

"I see." Captain Lewis looked at the other men. "Did you men see the buffalo running through camp?"

They all nodded.

"Was it wearing moccasins on its hooves?"

Colter whispered to Shannon, "Looks like we're in for some more of that *boudin blanc.*"

June 1, 1805
Our passage has been very difficult the past few days. It is
cold and rainy. On either side of us are enormous white
cliffs. There is no shore to speak of below the cliffs, and what
little ground there is, is so slippery the men have to take off
their moccasins while they use the towlines to pull the
pirogues through. Their feet have been terribly cut up by the
sharp rocks. They spend a good deal of the day up to their
armpits in the icy water, pulling the boats. Tomorrow I will
take a party of men ashore to shoot buffalo and elks. I need
the skins to stretch over the iron frame of our new boat....

I look at Drouillard to see if he remembers this
day. If he does, he shows no sign of it.

CAPTAIN LEWIS had taken a number of men ashore with
him, including Drouillard and Charbonneau, who had

once again gotten back into the Captain's good graces with a plateful of *boudin blanc*.

The men split up into pairs and I decided to ramble with Drouillard and Charbonneau. Drouillard shot three elk and two buffalo. Charbonneau missed four buffalo and two elk. We were headed back to camp with the skins when White Feather showed up.

"*Caw! Caw! Caw!*"

Drouillard and Charbonneau payed no attention to White Feather, but I knew better than to ignore his warnings. I stopped, put my nose up in the air, and picked up the scent of a grizzly coming our way. I started barking.

"Shut up, dog!" Charbonneau said.

I paid him no mind.

Drouillard looked in the direction I was facing. "Is your gun charged?" He asked Charbonneau.

"Of course it is."

"Good. I suspect you're going to need it presently. If I'm not mistaken, this is Sea's bear bark."

Charbonneau's eyes bulged. "Where?"

"There." Drouillard pointed to a small rise in the distance. The grizzly was just topping it. The wind was blowing our scent in his direction and he stood up to get a better whiff. "Here he comes." Drouillard dropped his skins and unslung his rifle.

The grizzly ran straight at us. Charbonneau looked

as if he might explode with fear. When the grizzly was a hundred yards away Charbonneau fired his rifle into the air.

"What do you think you're doing?" Drouillard asked, without taking his eyes off the charging bear.

Charbonneau was too frightened to answer.

"Better reload your gun," Drouillard said. "And make it quick."

Charbonneau ran. I wanted to join him but wasn't about to leave Drouillard alone.

"Guess I'm going to have to make this shot count," Drouillard said calmly. He waited until the grizzly was fifty feet away before firing. The bear reared back on its haunches and was dead before it hit the ground. "Think I hit it in the eye."

The left eye, as it turned out.

June 3, 1805
We are camped at a fork in the Missouri. One of the
branches appears to flow from the west, while the other flows
from the south. Unfortunately the Hidatsas, who have been
here before us, did not mention this second river and I do not
know which one leads to the Great Falls. I sent two teams to
scout ahead. They just reported in. Their opinion is that the
right branch is the Missouri and the left branch is another
river. The men's belief is based on the direction from which
the right branch flows and on the color of the water, which is
same color as the water we have been traveling on.

Captain Clark and I believe that the left branch is the
correct river. The river stones in the left branch are typical of
those found in rivers flowing directly from the mountains, as
is the color of the water, which is somewhat clearer in the left
branch.

If we take the wrong river there is a good chance we will
perish this winter....

CAPTAIN CLARK walked into the lodge and sat down. "What do you think, Meriwether?"

"Let's look at the map again."

Captain Clark unrolled the map of the river the Hidatsas had helped him draw at Fort Mandan. It did not show a fork in the Missouri. "How far do you think we are from the Great Falls?"

"I thought we were close, but now I'm not sure. I expected the scouts to find it today. If we follow the wrong river we will not find the Shoshones and their horses, which means we will not get over the mountains before winter."

"We have to get over those mountains before the snow comes," Captain Clark said. "What do you suggest?"

"I think our only choice is to scout farther up both rivers. Tomorrow I'll lead a team up the right branch for a day and a half. You'll lead a team up the left for the same amount of time. One of us is bound to find the Falls."

Early the next morning we headed up the right branch, which Captain Lewis named Maria's River, after his cousin Maria. With us were Drouillard, Sergeant Pryor, and Privates Shields, Windsor, Cruzatte, and Lepage.

The shore along the river was covered in prickly pear, which slowed our progress considerably.

After a day and a half of painful walking, the

Captain still wasn't sure, so we continued on another half day. That evening he concluded that the river could not be the Missouri because it appeared to flow too far to the north.

"I don't know as I agree with you, Captain," Sergeant Pryor said. "I think the Falls are still up ahead, but I won't be sorry to turn back. This place feels like bad luck to me."

He was not alone in thinking this.

"It's going to be pretty slow going with all these skins we're carrying," Cruzatte added. Along the way the men had shot several deer and elk and were carrying the skins on their sore backs for the Captain's iron boat.

"I have a solution for that," Captain Lewis said. "We'll build two rafts and let the river do our work for us."

The river worked against us, destroying both rafts minutes after we launched them. We ended up on the opposite shore.

"Told you this place was bad luck," Pryor said. He and the other men began drying out their gear.

"Drouillard and I will scout ahead and see how the route along this side is," Captain Lewis said.

I went with them. The north bank was blanketed with prickly pear and covered with impassable boulders. After half a mile it became clear that the shoreline could not be followed easily on foot. We returned to the men.

"We'll have to walk north to the prairie, then head back east and parallel the river," Captain Lewis said, removing prickly pear spines from my paw.

"With all these skins?"

"Regretfully, we will have to leave them behind."

That night on the prairie, a hard steady rain drenched us. We sat around a poor fire, shivering, wondering if the sun would ever rise again. This whole area put me on edge, and it wasn't because of the prickly pears or the difficult terrain. Ever since we got here the Captain seemed to have pulled into himself. I had seen him have minor bouts of melancholy along the trail, but the mood he was in now was far worse than before. I hoped he was right about the north branch not being the Missouri. I didn't want to come back this way again.

The next day we rejoined Maria's River farther downriver and slithered our way along a narrow trail above a steep hillside of slick clay. Captain Lewis slipped and nearly plunged a hundred feet into the river, but he managed to stop himself with his espontoon and crawl back up to the top. No sooner was he back on his feet than we heard Private Windsor behind us.

"God, Captain! What shall I do?"

Windsor was spread-eagled on the slippery hillside about fifteen feet below the trail. Captain Lewis was greatly alarmed at the private's predicament, but he did not show it.

The Captain got as close to the edge as he dared and smiled down at Windsor. "You're doing just fine," he said. "You're in no immediate danger." The statements were baldfaced lies, but Windsor believed both of them. He smiled and seemed relieved. "Take your knife and dig a foothold in the clay for your foot."

Windsor reached down with his knife and began digging the hole. The only thing holding him in place was the Captain's confidence.

"That's it," the Captain said. "Careful, now."

"How's that?" Windsor asked.

"Perfect! Now slip your right moccasin off and stick your bare foot in the hole. That's right. Just drop the moccasin. Now all you have to do is to crawl forward, using your knife to pull yourself up."

Windsor crawled up the slick clay face like a blowfly on a windowpane. When he got within an arm's length of the top, the Captain and Drouillard pulled him up over the edge.

"Guess I got a bit overwrought down there," said Windsor sheepishly. "Sorry, Captain."

"You responded just about right, Private Windsor."

We arrived back at the fork two days late.

"We were just about ready to send a search party out for you," Captain Clark said.

"We had a little trouble." Captain Lewis shook his head and sat down heavily on a buffalo skin. He had not been feeling well since our drenching on the prairie.

"Did you find the Great Falls?" Captain Lewis asked.

Captain Clark shook his head. "I assume you didn't, either."

"No. And the river veers too far to the north to be the Missouri. How does the left branch look?"

"We didn't get very far up it, but I think it's the Missouri."

"And the men?"

"They disagree."

The following morning Captain Lewis, still ill, tried to convince the men that the left branch was the Missouri River. He showed them several maps, arguing his case for nearly an hour.

"It doesn't matter to me whether you're right or wrong, Captain," Colter said when Captain Lewis finished. "I can't speak for the others, but I'll follow you and Captain Clark whatever direction you choose. The way I figure it, we are in this together."

"Well put, Colter."

"I'm with the captains, too."

"Count me in."

All the men were of the same mind, which cheered Captain Lewis considerably.

June 9, 1805
I am gratified at the men's willingness to follow us despite their belief we have chosen the wrong river. I pray that we are right.

To reach the mountains before winter we will travel light and fast. To this end we left the red pirogue at the fork and will pick it up on our way home. We also left a cache of supplies there.

I am leading a land party to reach the Great Falls ahead of the others. Drouillard, J. Fields, Gibson, and Goodrich are with me. If the Falls are not up this river, we may still have time to go back down and ascend the other branch and reach the mountains before winter. Captain Clark is follow-ing on the river with the others.

I am still not feeling well. When I left this morning Sacagawea was also ill....

THE CAPTAIN SLEPT very little our first night out be-cause of his illness. Despite this, we were on our way again early the next morning.

A few hours after we started, the men shot four elk.

"Butcher the meat and hang what we don't need next to the river," Captain Lewis said, sitting down heavily on the ground. He was pale and very weak. He leaned against a tree and closed his eyes. I lay down next to him until the scent of those elk guts pulled me away.

When I got my fill, I returned to the Captain and found him sleeping peacefully. Rather than disturb him, I joined Private Goodrich at the river, where he was fishing. He pulled out one lively fish after another with his pole and string. It was great fun to catch the flopping fish he threw onto the bank and bring them to him. Each time I brought one, he patted me on the head, took the fish from my mouth, and put it onto the growing pile.

"They don't call you Seaman for nothin'."

"Goodrich!"

It was Captain Lewis. I ran to him, with Goodrich right on my heels. The Captain was doubled over on the ground, clutching his stomach. "Gather...some... chokecherry...branches," he said through clenched teeth. "I need to make some medicine out of the bark."

Goodrich ran off. I had never seen the Captain in such pain and I wanted to help him, but there was nothing I could do but watch. Goodrich returned with the branches.

"What should I do with them, Captain?"

"Strip the bark...make tea..."

The men were alarmed at the Captain's condition. Drouillard wanted to find Captain Clark and bring him up, but Captain Lewis wouldn't let him, insisting that he would be fine after the tea had a chance to work.

By eight o'clock the Captain was sitting. By ten o'clock he was walking. He went to sleep about eleven, and the next morning he seemed perfectly recovered.

"Bless my mother for teaching me about herbs," he said. "Shall we proceed on, gentlemen?"

We walked nearly thirty miles before the Captain called a halt, saying that he was somewhat weakened from his ailment the day before. After we made camp the Captain worked on his notes, then did some fishing using a deer spleen as bait, which worked tolerably well.

The following day we came upon a vast plain with more buffalo than we had ever seen before. In the distance there was a great rumbling noise. Captain Lewis ran toward the sound.

June 13, 1805
O the Joy! We have arrived at the Great Falls and their
beauty is beyond my ability to put into words....

Colter flips through the red book. "Some pages are
missing here. You were there, Drouillard. Any idea
what was on them?"

Drouillard shakes his head.

I know....

THE CAPTAIN stood on the edge of the precipice, staring
across that grand crack in the prairie.

"A rainbow," he said, and began to weep.

The rainbow stretched from one side of the Falls to
the other. The sound of the water was deafening. The
cool mist drenched us.

It was not the beauty alone that moved him. Finding

the Great Falls meant the Shoshones were not far ahead.

The men came up and were as joyful as the Captain at the sight.

"You were right, Captain Lewis," Joe Fields said, staring in awe at the roaring spectacle.

"The important thing to me, Private Fields, is that you followed us. I value that more than this sublime sight."

The Captain stayed at the Falls while the men set up camp a short distance away. For over two hours he tried to capture the magnificent Falls by sketching them in the red book. The renderings looked pretty good to me, but each time he finished a sketch he tore the page from the red book and crumpled it in frustration.

Later that evening he used the pages to start his campfire.

June 14, 1805
I would give just about anything to be an artist. I thought
about it all last night. I fear no one will believe the sights we
have seen because of my inability to record them with any
accuracy. If I had only pursued this skill in my younger
years... but there is nothing that can be done now.

I followed the river last evening and found there are five
beautiful falls, not one. Our portage around them is going to
take considerable effort....

CAPTAIN LEWIS sent Joe Fields downriver with a letter
for Captain Clark, telling him we had found the Falls
and suggesting a location for the lower portage camp.
Then he and I set off for a ramble.

We walked past the Falls, which the Captain was
particularly drawn to. There was a small island between
two of the upper falls. In the center of the island was a

dead tree towering above the others with a gigantic bird nest perched in the top branches.

"Bald eagle."

A large black bird with a white head and a yellow beak sat on the edge of the nest feeding her brood. We were close enough to see the downy eaglets open their black beaks for the food she offered. The Captain brought out the red book and tried to capture this scene, but again he ended up ripping pages out of his journal.

"Let's go, Sea. I'm more skillful with a rifle than I am with a pen."

We walked up to the last falls, from where we could see an immense flat prairie cut in two by the meandering Missouri River. Ahead of us was a smaller river that flowed into the Missouri, with a thousand buffalo grazing next to its shore.

"Perhaps we should shoot some dinner in case we don't have time to make it back to camp before dark."

A brisk wind blew toward us. Not being able to pick up our scent, the buffaloes continued to graze, unconcerned at our approach. The Captain picked a young cow out of the group. He steadied his rifle on his espontoon and fired. She was hit squarely, but she didn't fall over. The herd moved a short distance away from her and continued grazing. As we watched her bleeding out, the fur on my back came to attention. I turned my head.

There was a grizzly behind us, not twenty steps away. My barking brought him up on his hind legs. Captain Lewis snapped his rifle to his shoulder and pulled the trigger. There was a sickening *click*. He had forgotten to reload after he shot the buffalo.

"Run, Sea!"

The grizzly was right on our heels. We ran to the river. The Captain splashed into the water up to his waist, then turned around and pointed his espontoon at the grizzly. I thought surely the bear would come in after us, but when he saw the espontoon he skidded to a stop, turned, and ran away.

"That was a bit of good luck."

That was a miracle. The grizzly continued to run, glancing back every once in a while to make sure we weren't chasing him.

"I think we'll leave the buffalo cow for Mister Grizzly."

We rambled over the smaller river and explored it for a few hours. On our way back across the prairie an animal we hadn't seen before came out of its burrow and snarled at us. It looked like a cross between a wolf and a cat. Captain Lewis fired at it, but it disappeared back into its den and didn't come out again.

We hadn't taken three hundred steps from the den when two bull buffalo charged us.

"I don't think they know what we are," Captain Lewis said. "Let's have some fun, Sea." He walked right at the charging buffalo. As soon as they got close enough to see we were a man and dog, they reeled around and ran away.

"It appears that all the beasts in the neighborhood are in league to destroy us." Captain Lewis chuckled. "Perhaps we should head back to camp before our luck sours."

I think this was among the happiest days the Captain ever had.

June 16, 1805
This afternoon I rejoined Captain Clark below the Falls
and found Sacagawea gravely ill. After a battle of wills, I
finally prevailed upon her to swallow some of our medicine,
although I am not convinced it will do her any good....

"I DON'T KNOW what else to do," Captain Lewis said. He looked down at Bird Woman. She was finally asleep.

Captain Clark cradled Pomp in his arms. "What do you think she has?"

"I wish I knew. Stomach cramps, fever, no appetite... it could be anything. If the fever does not break soon, we're going to lose her."

"I want to take her home," Charbonneau said.

Captain Lewis looked at him like he had lost his mind. "Home?"

"To the Hidatsa village."

The Captain pushed Charbonneau out of the lodge so they wouldn't disturb Bird Woman.

"Listen, you old fool. Your wife is in no condition to travel. She can't even stand! If she died along the way, what would happen to your son? How would you feed him?"

"Begging your pardon, Captain. But the only reason you want her to continue on is for her to help you get your horses."

Captain Lewis flushed in anger, and for a moment I thought he might strike Charbonneau. He took a deep breath. "We have grown very fond of your wife and son," he said slowly. "My only concern is for their safety. I will do everything in my power to save her, but if you ever accuse me of jeopardizing a member of this party to accomplish my goal, there is nothing on earth that will save you, Mister Charbonneau!"

Charbonneau took several steps backward.

"Do I make myself clear?"

Charbonneau nodded and Captain Lewis went back into the lodge.

The captains spent the evening in the lodge tending Bird Woman and discussing how to make the sixteen-mile portage around the falls.

"We'll have to leave the white pirogue here," Captain Lewis said. "It will be hard enough to get the smaller dugouts overland."

"I'll have the men begin making carts for the dug-outs tomorrow," Captain Clark said. "I guess when we get above the Falls we'll have to make more dugouts to carry—"

"We shouldn't need them," Captain Lewis interrupted. "We have the iron boat. There's an island above the Falls that will be perfect to put it together. We can start portaging the pieces first thing in the morning. I'll have the boat floating by the time all our supplies are on the island."

Captain Clark was not nearly as optimistic about the iron boat as Captain Lewis. "Sacagawea seems to be showing some improvement," he commented, changing the subject.

"She's not out of danger, but you're right—she does appear to be getting better."

June 23, 1806
I write this from our camp on the island above the Great
Falls. I have named this White Bear Island because of the
number of grizzlies in the neighborhood. Although we
are five miles away from the nearest falls, we can hear their
roar.

We have stored the white pirogue and made another
cache of supplies at the lower portage camp for when we
return.

The boat frame arrived today and I have enlisted
J. Fields, Sergeant Gass, and John Shields to assist me in
putting it together. The boat is 36 feet long and should serve
our purposes admirably once it's afloat. I overheard a few of
the men referring to my boat as the "experiment" the other
day. They don't seem to believe the boat will float, but I'm
confident they are in error, just as they were about the true
course of the Missouri.

The greatest challenge now is finding a sealant to

waterproof the seams of the skins. If I had known that find-
ing pitch for this purpose was going to be so hard in this
area, I would have collected it downriver and brought it with
us. I am experimenting with a new sealant made of charcoal
and tallow, which we have used with great success in the past
to patch our canoes....

CAPTAIN LEWIS'S greatest challenge was his iron boat, but my greatest challenge was the grizzlies. White Bear Island was crawling with them. During the day they kept their distance, but at night while the men slept they became bolder. The men slept with rifles loaded and fires burning brightly, but I think it was my angry barking that kept the bears away.

The men's greatest challenge was getting the canoes and supplies around the Falls. The ground was steep, covered with prickly pear, and rutted with dried buffalo tracks that were as sharp as arrows. The men pushed and pulled the heavy carts over this rough ground an inch at a time. Every few feet they had to stop and rest. When they lay down they fell asleep, and Captain Clark had to kick them to wake them up. Of all the hardships they had suffered on our journey, this portage was by far the worst. On some days, when the wind was blow-ing right, they were able to raise the sail on the canoes, which eased their burden a little. But on most days the weather did not help matters. Strong winds, thunder, lightning, rain, and hail assaulted the men, adding to their labor.

When Captain Clark left White Bear Island to retrieve the last dugout canoe, I went with him. I doubt Captain Lewis even noticed when I left. The only thing on his mind was readying the iron boat.

York, Bird Woman, and Pomp accompanied us across the windy plain to the lower portage camp. A few miles before we got there we were caught in a terrible rain-and-hail storm. We took shelter in a deep gully. Bird Woman unstrapped Pomp from his cradleboard, stripped off his wet clothes, and started to dry him as best as she could. Then we heard the water. A second later it was upon us.

"Flash flood!" Captain Clark shouted. "Climb!" He grabbed Pomp and handed him up to York, then took Bird Woman by the arm and dragged her up behind him.

The water swept me away, pushing me a hundred yards down the gully before I was able to clamber out onto the prairie, where I was greeted by wind-driven hail the size of musket balls.

"Run to stay warm!" Captain Clark shouted above the blasts of thunder.

When we arrived at the lower camp, we found men as naked as little Pomp, huddled around the fires trying to dry their clothes. They were covered with bruises and cuts from the pounding hail.

July 4, 1805
Our country's 29th birthday. To celebrate we poured
the last of our whiskey, and the men are having a merry
time by the sound of it.

I am very discouraged this evening. The boat is taking
much longer than I thought. With rain and hail every day,
the skins will not dry. I am worried we will not find the
Shoshones. Worried we will not make it over the mountains
before winter....

CAPTAIN LEWIS was sitting near the iron boat with the
red book in his lap, his pen in his hand, and his last
glass of whiskey at his side when Captain Clark found
him.

"I wondered where you had gotten to. What are you
doing down here by yourself?"

"I'm afraid I'm not very good company this evening."

Captain Clark sat down next to him. "What's on your mind, Meriwether?"

"Nothing, really."

"How long will you give the boat?"

"What do you mean?"

"How long will you wait before we push on without it?"

"You don't think it will work, either?" Captain Lewis was clearly surprised.

"It was a good idea," Captain Clark said carefully. "But no, I don't think she'll float."

"The boat will work! All we have to do is seal the seams and she'll take us all the way to the Pacific."

"Providing there's an easy portage to a navigable river, which you know there may not be."

"Have you lost faith in the Northwest Passage?"

"A little," Captain Clark admitted. "Those mountains are much bigger than we expected."

"Regardless," Captain Lewis said, "we'll sail this boat as far as we can."

The captains sat in silence for a long time.

"I've been thinking I should take a large party out hunting," Captain Clark said. "The Hidatsas warned us that there are few buffalo above the Falls. We'll need extra meat to get over the mountains."

"Give me the men for a few more days," Captain Lewis said. "The skins are nearly completed."

"Of course." Captain Clark stood. "I hope I'm wrong about the boat, Meriwether, but if for some reason it doesn't work, you can't blame yourself."

July 8, 1805
I believe the sealant we're using for the boat will work ad-
mirably until we get to the mountains, where there will be
trees with the type of pitch we need to do the job right.

Captain Clark has taken most of the men on a hunting
expedition. My boat should be ready to float by to-
morrow....

I JOINED CAPTAIN CLARK and discovered he was not
looking only for meat. As soon as we got out onto the
prairie he divided the men and took his small party to
the Medicine River.

"While you're hunting you might keep your eyes
open for trees that are big enough to make canoes."

"And animal specimens for Captain Lewis," added
Drouillard. "You know how new creatures cheer
him up."

The men knew. They also knew that the iron boat was not going to work and the Captain would need something to distract him from the failure.

We returned that evening with a kit fox and a live squirrel. Captain Lewis barely looked at the new animals, saying he would get to them later when he had more time.

The next afternoon Captain Lewis launched his experiment. The boat wasn't in the water more than five minutes before almost every seam split in two. It quickly filled with water and settled on the shallow river bottom. The only person who seemed surprised was Captain Lewis.

He waded out to the iron boat and examined several seams. No one spoke. When he got back on shore he walked over to Captain Clark and said, "We'll have to make canoes."

"I'll go out tomorrow morning and see if we can find suitable trees," Captain Clark said, not mentioning that he had already marked several for this purpose.

"While you're doing that we'll dismantle the boat and bury it with anything else we don't need. I'm going for a ramble. Let's go, Sea."

This was the hardest ramble I ever took with the Captain. A mile away from camp he started mumbling to himself. A half mile farther he started shouting.

"Fool! Idiot! The men knew the boat would sink, but your pride made you deaf to their logic. You delayed the party by two weeks. Those two wasted weeks just might kill every man!"

He continued on like this for another mile. I lagged behind him several yards. Seeing him act like this was more frightening than any of my encounters with grizzlies.

We came to a small stand of trees. The Captain, still berating himself, picked a heavy limb up off the ground and began bashing it against a tree trunk over and over and over again until he was too weak to swing. He fell to his knees and covered his face with his bloodied hands.

I lay twenty feet away shivering with worry. After a very long time, the Captain quieted and looked up with red-rimmed eyes. He looked right at me but didn't see me. He took several chest-heaving breaths, then lay back against the tree he had beaten and fell asleep.

Because of the grizzlies, White Bear Island was probably the worst place in the world to take a nap alone. I kept my eyes and nose open for trouble, and that's when I saw White Feather. I wanted to run over to him, but I felt that my place was next to the Captain. Directly below White Feather stood Drouillard, calmly scanning the flat prairie with his rifle cradled in his thick arms.

The Captain slept for a long time. When he awoke he was better, but still not himself. We walked back to camp and found Captain Clark in the lodge scratching in his journal by dim candlelight.

Captain Lewis looked around the lodge and saw Bird Woman, Pomp, and Charbonneau fast asleep under their blanket. Drouillard was not lying in his regular spot. "Where's Drouillard?"

Captain Clark looked up from his journal. "He said he was going to sleep out with the men tonight."

This was the first and last time I ever heard Captain Clark tell an outright lie to Captain Lewis. He knew Drouillard had followed us.

"That's strange."

"Charbonneau made *boudin blanc* tonight," Captain Clark said. "We saved some for you." He uncovered the plate.

Captain Lewis looked at the sausage. "I don't recall getting angry with Charbonneau today." Captain Lewis took a bite of sausage. "William, the next time you catch me doing something prideful like this boat, for god's sake please stop me."

Captain Clark grinned. "I'll try." He put his journal away and got under his blanket.

Captain Lewis gave me a sausage link and finished the rest himself.

Early the next morning Captain Clark took some

men to the Medicine River to make canoes. The men who remained sewed new moccasins, dried meat, and packed supplies. In the afternoon Captain Lewis had them disassemble the iron boat and bury the pieces in a hole like they were old bones.

July 15, 1805
Once again we are moving west. The canoes are heavily
loaded and several of the men must walk alongshore, as there
is no room for them in the boats. If only I could have gotten
the iron boat to work! But that is in the past and I need to
let that failure go....

BUT THE CAPTAIN could not seem to let it go. When we were alone on rambles he still talked about the boat, which led him to talking about other failures, until it seemed like he had never succeeded at anything in his entire life. He talked of the times he drank too much and said things he should have held inside. How he had left his mother and brother to manage their property and holdings because he could not contain his lust to wander. His failure to find a woman who could love him as he loved her. The list was long, but none of these failures seemed to amount to much to me compared to everything he had accomplished in his life. He was a skilled botanist, biologist, woodsman, hunter, and tracker, and a wonderful commander. He had successfully led a group of men almost all the way across the continent into lands never before seen by his tribe. And he was only thirty years old.

The day after we left White Bear Island, Captain Lewis led Potts, Lepage, and Drouillard ahead of the canoes to hunt and get a better look at the mountains.

Once again food was scarce, but young geese were plentiful and I thought they would be easy for me to catch as they could not fly yet. I came across a flock and gave chase. As I was about to put my mouth on one of the downy morsels, a bold mother goose descended upon me and showed me that her wings were used for more than flying. She pummeled me with them and bit my ears until I was nearly senseless. I gave up trying to catch her pup and ran for my life. She pursued me with her feathered fists nearly a quarter mile upriver before she decided I had been punished enough. The men laughed so hard at the sight, they had to sit down where they stood. Even Captain Lewis managed to smile, an expression I hadn't seen for a while. The beating I'd taken was worth that little smile of his.

Late that afternoon we got a good look at the Rockies, and it was a sobering sight. The snow-capped mountains were immense.

"How are we going to get over them?" Potts asked.

"We will," the Captain said, but at that moment he didn't look very confident. "We have to. We'll camp here and wait for the boats."

The Captain stared at the white peaks for hours that afternoon and seemed to barely breathe as he took them in. I was reminded of how he had stared at the iron boat a few days before she sank. I hoped we wouldn't suffer the same fate.

When the sun set, the white peaks changed to pink and purple. "They are beautiful," the Captain said. "But deadly. We need those horses."

Captain Clark and the boats arrived midmorning the next day. The captains sat a short distance from the men, looking at the mountains, talking about how to cross over them before winter set in.

"We need horses," Captain Lewis said. "We should have encountered the Shoshones by now."

"Maybe we're scaring them off," Captain Clark suggested.

"What do you mean?"

"Our guns. Maybe they've heard our guns and are hiding themselves. From what we've been told, the Shoshones have never seen white men."

The Captain thought about this for a time before responding. "What do you suggest?"

"I'll take a small party ahead with as much food as we can carry, so we don't have to hunt and fire our guns.

We'll try to find the Shoshones and convince them we mean them no harm before the main party arrives."

"And you want me to command the boats?" What Captain Lewis meant was that he was usually the rambling captain and Clark was generally the water captain. I think he was hoping Captain Clark would see this as clearly as he did, but Captain Clark didn't see it this way at all.

"The water along here should not present a problem."

Captain Lewis saw his friend's determination and didn't argue the point. "When will you leave?"

"Early tomorrow morning. I'll take Joe Fields, Private Potts, and York. We will find the Shoshones."

"I hope you do."

Captain Clark smiled and walked off toward camp to tell the men to ready themselves.

Captain Lewis scratched my head. "Guess we're going back on the water, mate."

July 19, 1805
The canoes are making fair time, and as Captain Clark
predicted, we have had little trouble, but I would prefer to be
in his place looking for the Shoshones.

Today we passed through spires of black gloomy rock
looming at least 1,200 feet above the river. I named them the
gates of the Rocky Mountains.

My dog is suffering greatly from a small seed found
along this part of the river....

I HAD GOTTEN used to the swarms of gnats and mosquitoes and the blood-sucking ticks. Even the prickly pear was tolerable if the Captain got the spines out of me before they festered. But those evil little seeds caused me unending misery.

When I tried to scratch the seeds out, they burrowed deeper into my fur and bit my skin like red fire ants. And jumping into the cold water was no relief. There was only one solution for my misery—Captain Lewis spent half the night cutting the seeds out of my fur with his knife, making me as bald as the top of Charbonneau's head in some places.

"These seeds have barbs so the animals passing by pick them up in their fur," Captain Lewis said as he sliced away. "This disperses the seeds to new areas where they can germinate." *Slice.* "Rather like hitching a ride on a wagon." *Slice.*

At that moment I couldn't have cared less about the seeds' clever mode of travel. If the Captain hadn't been there to cut them out, I would have scratched myself to death.

"I'm confining you to one of the canoes, Sea." *Slice.* "At least until we get through this seed area." *Slice.* "I can't spend every night doing this." *Slice.*

That was fine with me. *Slice.*

Our passage over the next few days was very difficult, and the men suffered greatly from their hard labor. They had to pull the canoes with elk-hide ropes, and in the shallower areas push the canoes against the current with poles.

About the only encouragement the men had during this time came on the day we passed a section of the river that Sacagawea recognized. She claimed that her tribe was not too far ahead.

On that same day we caught up with Captain Clark

and his small party. They had been slowed by the rough terrain and the condition of Captain Clark's feet, which had been badly injured by prickly pear. As soon as we set up camp, Captain Lewis warmed some water in a pot and cleaned Captain Clark's swollen feet.

"You'll not get far on these, William."

"My feet will be fine," Captain Clark said, wincing in pain.

"They will heal much faster resting in one of the canoes. I would be happy to take your place."

"I said my feet will be fine, Meriwether! I will not be coddled. We're heading out again early tomorrow morning." He hobbled painfully into the lodge.

July 27, 1805
We arrived at the Three Forks this morning. I named the
southeast fork after Albert Gallatin, our secretary of the
treasury. The middle fork I am calling the Madison River,
after James Madison, our secretary of state. And the
right fork, which is the river we will follow to the Rocky
Mountains, I am calling the Jefferson River, in honor
of our president.

We traveled a short distance up the Jefferson and came
to a small island, where I found a note from Captain Clark
saying he would return to this spot soon and to wait for him
here. I am not sorry to wait, as the men could use a rest....

CAPTAIN CLARK limped into camp that same afternoon
and collapsed in front of our lodge. His face was the
color of ash and it was a wonder he could even stand on
his feet in the condition they were in.

Captain Lewis took the bloody moccasins off his

friend's feet and cleaned the infected ulcers with warm water.

"You're running a fever," Captain Lewis said. "We'll rest here a few days. Then I'll take some men ahead and look for the Shoshones."

Captain Clark was too weak to object.

July 30, 1805
We are under way once again. Captain Clark is still suffer-
ing, but the rest has revived the other men. They had good
luck hunting, and a chance to sew new moccasins to replace
their tattered ones, destroyed during the hard pull past the
gates of the Rocky Mountains.

This morning I walked alongshore with Charbonneau
and Sacagawea. We came to where Sacagawea was captured
by the Hidatsas. She showed us the stand of trees she and
her friend ran toward. They had almost made their escape
when…

"I FELL AND TWISTED my ankle," Bird Woman said. "It
was here." She bent down and touched the root of a tree
sticking out of the ground. "My friend Jumping Fish
came back and tried to help me, but the ankle would
not hold my weight. We heard horses coming behind
us. I pushed Jumping Fish away and told her to save

herself. She didn't want to leave me, but she made herself go, looking back at me one last time before she disappeared into the trees." Bird Woman turned and pointed behind her. "The two mounted Hidatsas came from the river, their faces painted red, each with a wet scalp tied to his belt.

"The first warrior jumped from his horse before it came to a stop. He grabbed my hair, jerked my head off the ground, and screamed. My brother came running from the trees and knocked the warrior down. He shouted for me to run, not realizing my foot was injured. I crawled toward the trees, but before I reached them, I was picked up by another warrior. He threw me across his horse."

"And your brother?" Captain Lewis asked quietly.

Bird Woman shook her head. "I'm sure he was killed. There were many Hidatsas and their blood was up. As the warrior carried me away I saw many people killed. Those who ran were clubbed like buffalo. I saw with my own eyes four men, four old women, and several young boys killed. The young women, like me, were spared."

In the afternoon Charbonneau and Sacagawea rejoined the canoes and Captain Lewis and I continued on alone. In order to avoid the swampy areas created by beaver dams, we had to walk inland some distance before we could proceed upriver. When we reached the river again

Captain Lewis could not tell whether we were above or below the canoes. He fired his rifle twice, hoping to hear return fire and determine the direction to travel, but there was no report. My nose told me we were ahead of the canoes, but there was no way to convey this to the Captain. Rather than hazard a guess, he shot a duck, built a fire, and decided to spend the night.

I sniffed around and discovered that a grizzly had walked by our camp not long before we arrived. I stayed alert all night long, but the only visitor we had was a deer who left her bed early and came down to the river for a drink of water. By sunrise I was tired and very hungry. I needed more than a pile of duck bones to fill my stomach.

"We'll wait here a while longer, then head upriver." The Captain took his journal out and began scratching in it. I headed downriver to see if I could find breakfast and the other men before the Captain led us farther away. I didn't find any food, but I did find Charbonneau walking by himself and making more noise than a grizzly bear. He appeared to be having an argument with Bird Woman, although she was nowhere in sight. This was not unusual. During the journey I had seen nearly all the men have these one-sided conversations.

"What about Pomp?" Charbonneau asked the river. "Don't you care about our child? If we find your people, we'll spend the winter with them. If these foolish men survive the mountains—and I doubt they will—we can rejoin the party in the spring and return to the east with them. It's our only course!"

Charbonneau stopped and looked at a tree as if it were saying something to him. The full cheeks above his gray beard turned bright red and his eyes bulged as if the tree were insulting him.

"You are a bad wife and a bad mother. You will do what I say!" Knowing Bird Woman, I thought it wise that he said this to a tree and not to her. She was gentle, but she did not put up with silliness, especially her husband's.

"I'll not risk my only son…What's that?" Charbonneau laughed. "The Pacific Ocean is nothing but a big lake filled with stinking water. It's not worth risking our lives to see it. Besides, the only reason the captains allowed you to come with me is because you speak Shoshone. After we get the horses they'll have no use for you." He smiled and put his hand out toward the invisible Bird Woman. "Don't cry…Someday I'll take you to the Pacific Ocean."

I had never seen Bird Woman shed a single tear, although she'd had reason enough to do so on many occasions.

Charbonneau sighed with satisfaction, well pleased with his one-way conversation. He continued upriver, walking right past me as if I were as invisible as Bird Woman. It occurred to me to run up behind him and bark to see how high he could jump, but I didn't. He might have shot me, or more likely himself. Instead I swung around him and rejoined Captain Lewis, who was just about ready to leave.

"I wondered where you had gotten to, Sea. We better go up and find the others before they get too far ahead."

I sat down.

"Let's go."

I barked and ran a short distance downriver.

"What's gotten into you?"

About this time Charbonneau appeared around the bend. "Captain Lewis!" he shouted.

The Captain waved. I ran back to him.

"You're a fine dog, Sea. A fine dog." He scratched me behind the ear. "What brings you out here so early, Mister Charbonneau?"

"I was concerned about you, Captain. I thought I'd walk ahead of the others and see if I could find you. I'm delighted you are all right."

The Captain looked at him doubtfully. "How are the men?"

"Not good. Five are very sick and Captain Clark's feet are still in a bad way."

Without another word the Captain started walking downriver. Charbonneau tried to match his vigorous pace but could not do it without wheezing at the effort. "I...was...wondering...uh...if I could discuss...something...with you."

"Go ahead," Captain Lewis said without slowing down.

"It's...about...Sacagawea...and—"

"Yes?"

"Uh..."

"What is it, Charbonneau?"

"Never mind...I'll see you back at the canoes."

We left Charbonneau with his hands on his knees trying to catch his breath.

July 31, 1805

After reuniting with the party this morning I continued to walk onshore. Our situation is dire. A number of men are sick and I don't feel entirely well myself—some kind of stomach disorder seems to be going through our group. Despite this I must march ahead with a few of the men and find the Shoshones. I'll leave tomorrow morning with Sergeant Gass, Drouillard, and Charbonneau, who nearly begged me to let him join us. I told him he could accompany us under the condition that he keep up. Sacagawea asked if she could go as well, but I told her no. I am afraid she would slow us down with Pomp on her back....

"I GUESS WE'RE READY," Captain Lewis said. He had just finished wrapping Captain Clark's ankle with a clean bandage. "Try to keep this dry if you can."

"Thank you, Meriwether. Godspeed and be careful."

"We will." Captain Lewis turned to leave, then stopped and turned back. "If I'm not mistaken, Captain, today is your birthday."

"That is correct, sir."

"Is there anything you fancy for a present?"

"You know, a Shoshone horse would suit me just fine. In lieu of that, a fat elk roast would be tolerable."

Captain Lewis smiled. "A man should have a horse and a good meal on his birthday. I'll see what I can do on both accounts."

We did not find a horse that day, but the Captain and Drouillard each shot a fat elk. We left the meat next to the river where Captain Clark would see it.

On our second day out Charbonneau tried his hardest to keep up but fell farther and farther behind. When he finally trudged into camp that night the fires had burned down and Drouillard and Sergeant Gass were under their covers fast asleep.

Captain Lewis was awake, writing by the light of a candle. "There's some meat," he said.

Charbonneau's appetite had not suffered during his ordeal. He ate every scrap and gnawed the bones until they shone. When he finished he let out a long satisfied belch, then said in his labored English, "Captain, I'm glad we finally have this moment for a private conversation."

The Captain looked up from his journal. "What's on your mind, Charbonneau?"

"It's my wife, Sacagawea."

"I see."

"Let me get right to the point."

"If you would. I'm tired and we need to get an early start in the morning."

"Of course…well…after we meet with the Shoshones I'm wondering if you'll be needing Sacagawea any longer."

"First we have to find the Shoshones."

"My wife insists they are near here."

"I'm comforted. What do you want, Charbonneau?"

"Of course…uh…What I want is to winter with the Shoshones and meet up with you when you return."

"I see. And how does Sacagawea feel about this?"

"She and the boy will stay with me, of course."

"Of course." Captain Lewis pushed a stick into the embers. "I was under the impression that Sacagawea wanted to travel with us all the way to the Pacific."

"She's a stubborn woman!"

Captain Lewis chuckled. "Don't mistake stubbornness for strength."

"My real concern is for the boy." Charbonneau looked off into the darkness toward the west. "Those mountains."

"Pomp seems to fare better than any of us," the

Captain said. "I envy him sometimes, strapped to his mother, protected and fed...But if you want to stay on this side of the mountains, you may."

"Thank you, Captain," Charbonneau said. "But it will take more than your permission, I'm afraid."

"What do you mean?"

"Sacagawea will stay only if you and Captain Clark order us to stay."

"Ahhh, now I understand."

"I knew you would."

"But I cannot oblige you."

"Why not?"

"Because Sacagawea is a member of the Corps, just as you are. She has suffered along with us and she deserves to complete the journey if she chooses. I'll give you permission to stay, but I will not order you to stay or interfere in your private affairs unless it somehow threatens the others."

"But, Captain—"

"I'm going to sleep, Charbonneau. This subject is closed. And that is an order. Good night."

August 8, 1805
We walked ahead of the canoes for several days. Charbon-
neau slowed us down considerably, complaining that his feet
were sore. I gave him and Sergeant Gass our packs, and
Drouillard and I struck out ahead at a rapid pace. It was
to no avail, as we saw no sign of the Shoshones.

When we returned to the canoes we found everything in
disarray. Captain Clark's ankle is still in a bad way, though
the infection is draining steadily, and Private Shannon has
gotten himself lost once again. Drouillard and Reubin
Fields went out searching for him, but neither had any
luck.

Not far from here is a hill the Indians call the Beaver's
Head. Sacagawea tells us that this place is very near her
people's summer encampment. Tomorrow I will walk ahead
with Drouillard, Shields, and McNeal, and will not return
until I find the Shoshones....

SHANNON RETURNED the next morning. Once again he thought the main party was ahead of him and walked for several days upriver before realizing his mistake. He came back to camp with three deerskins, having fared much better than the last time he got lost.

Our small group proceeded on ahead of the canoes for two days and saw no Indians, but their scent was everywhere and I knew it was just a matter of time before we discovered them or they discovered us.

On the morning of the third day Captain Lewis decided to search the prairie for an Indian road, hoping it would lead us to the Shoshones. To cover more ground he sent Drouillard out to the right and Private Shields to the left. Private McNeal and I stayed in the middle with the Captain.

"If you find a road, put your hat on the barrel of your rifle and hold it above your head," the Captain instructed.

We hadn't gone far when I picked up the scent of a horse. It was very fresh. Nose to the ground, I started following it, getting more excited with every step as the scent became sharper.

"Hold it, Sea," the Captain said.

I looked back at him. He and McNeal had stopped and were shielding their eyes from the morning sun. Standing on a low rise a couple miles in front of us was a mounted Indian brave. Captain Lewis took his eagle eye out and aimed it at the horse and rider.

"He certainly has a different look about him and his horse is a magnificent specimen. I believe we have found a Shoshone." He handed the eagle eye to McNeal.

"What do you want to do, Captain?"

"We'll walk up to him and pray he doesn't run off."

We walked slowly toward the Indian, and after a while he started walking his horse toward us. Under his breath the Captain said, "That's it...We are friendly."

When we drew to within a mile of one another the Indian pulled his horse up. The Captain stopped, unrolled his blanket, raised it above his head three times, then spread it on the ground in front of him to signal his friendly intentions and his desire to trade. But the Indian did not seem interested in the Captain's invitation to sit on the blanket. He appeared to be staring at a point somewhere in back of us.

"What the devil is he looking at?" The Captain turned around. Drouillard and Shields were a mile behind, walking up on our flanks. "Fools! They're going to scare him off."

"I could try to holler at them to stop," McNeal offered.

"No! The brave might think we're up to something and leave." The Captain gave his rifle to McNeal and pulled out a handful of trinkets from his pack. "You wait here."

He advanced on the Indian and held the trinkets up in the air while shouting, *"Tab-ba-bone! Tab-ba-bone!"*

which he understood from Bird Woman was the Shoshone word for "white man." He drew to within two hundred paces, but the Indian still seemed more interested in Drouillard and Shields, who were gaining ground quickly. The Captain stopped and waved at the two men to stop. Drouillard stopped immediately, but Shields continued forward as if he had not seen the signal.

The Captain started forward again. *"Tab-ba-bone! Tab-ba-bone!"*

At 150 paces the Captain, now nearly frantic to get the warrior's attention on him and off Shields, pulled up the sleeve of his deerskin shirt to his elbow and pointed to his forearm, which had not been darkened by the sun. *"Tab-ba-bone!"*

At one hundred paces the Indian turned his horse around and whipped it. A moment later they were gone from view. Captain Lewis stopped and stared at the empty prairie in disbelief. Shields walked up to him without a clue that he had done anything wrong.

"Why didn't you stop?" Captain Lewis shouted.

"I didn't realize—"

"You may have just scared off our only hope of getting over the mountains alive, Private! That Indian is going to tell his tribe we're here and there is a good chance they will go into hiding, all because you were not paying attention. Do you understand?"

"Yes, sir, but—"

"All because a man was daydreaming!" The Captain threw the trinkets on the ground in disgust.

After spending a miserable night on the wet prairie without much in the way of food, we set out again the next morning. We found a well-traveled trail, which was encouraging, but after following it for twenty very hungry miles our hopes were all but gone. We had seen no game and no Shoshones, though I had been picking up their scent all day long.

That night the Captain and his men were very dejected, especially Private Shields.

"If there's a tribe of Shoshones around here," Drouillard commented, "I'd love to know what they are eating."

As soon as the men went to sleep I went in search of food and came back two hours later without so much as a mouse. What *were* the Shoshones eating?

It turned out they were eating roots. The following morning we spotted a group of two Indian women, an old man, and their skinny dogs in the distance. They were pushing long sticks into the ground, digging up plants. Captain Lewis gave his rifle to Shields and told the men to wait where they were.

The old man ran off as soon as he saw the Captain, and the women were not far behind. They disappeared behind a hill. The dogs were somewhat bolder. One of them slunk up to me. The Captain tried to grab it, but it scooted out of reach. The Captain wanted to tie a few trinkets around the dog's neck with a kerchief, hoping the Indians would see them and realize our intentions were good. He made a second lunge for the dog, but missed again. The dog ran away with his tail flat against his belly like a frightened prairie wolf.

The Captain signaled the men to join us. "We'll follow their tracks."

We hadn't been on the trail long when we suddenly came upon three different Indian women, not more than thirty paces away. One of them immediately ran. The remaining two, an old woman and a youngster, sat down on the ground and bowed their heads, trembling with fear. The Captain put his rifle down and slowly approached them.

"*Tab-ba-bone,*" he said quietly, trying to calm them. "*Tab-ba-bone.*" When he reached the old woman he gently encouraged her to stand. She did so, but her legs were shaking so badly they barely supported her frail body. "*Tab-ba-bone.*" The Captain pulled his sleeve up. "*Tab-ba-bone.*"

The old woman didn't understand what he was saying, but she was clearly curious about the white skin of his forearm. The Captain gave her some blue beads. The fear left her face and her legs stopped shaking.

The Captain called Drouillard over. "Ask her to call the girl who ran away. I suspect she's hiding nearby. I don't want her to run off and alarm the tribe until we have a chance to explain ourselves."

It took some fancy hand-talk, but Drouillard managed to get his meaning across. The old woman called out for the girl and a moment later she returned, out of breath from fear. Captain Lewis gave her a handful of beads, then painted all the women's faces with vermilion, a kind of red paint, which Bird Woman had said was a sign of peace to the Shoshones.

"Are they Shoshones?" Shields asked.

"I believe they are," the Captain said. Shields was very relieved. "Ask them to take us to their camp."

Drouillard made the signs and the old woman led us down the trail. We hadn't gone two miles when sixty mounted Shoshone warriors rode toward us at full speed. Hurriedly, before they reached us, Captain Lewis put his rifle down and pulled an American flag out of his pack. He held the flag over his head as he walked forward, followed by the old woman and two girls. When they got up to the riders, the old woman showed the chief the blue beads she had been given and explained that the Captain had come in peace.

The chief's stern face broke into a wide grin. He jumped off his horse and embraced the Captain, shouting, *"Ah-hi-e! Ah-hi-e!"* which I learned later meant "I am much pleased! Much rejoiced to see you!" The other Shoshones followed the chief's lead, jumping from their horses and hugging the Captain and the other men as if they were long-lost brothers. I even got a few pats and hugs.

Captain Lewis painted vermilion on their faces and the Indians responded by tying a few small seashells in the men's and my hair.

The Captain spread his blanket on the ground, started a parley, and passed the pipe around. The chief confirmed that he and his men were from the Shoshone tribe. He told us his name was Cameahwait. Captain Lewis gave him the American flag he was carrying.

August 15, 1805

We have finally found the Shoshones. They are friendly and have more than enough horses to get us over the mountains, but there isn't a scrap of meat in their camp. This morning we took half of our flour and mixed it with a few berries for breakfast. This we shared with Cameahwait and he was overjoyed with this pitiful meal. I'll delay here a few days to give Captain Clark a chance to reach the fork of the Jefferson River.

Drouillard and I met with Cameahwait and asked him about the route over the mountains. What he told me was very disturbing and I can only hope he is mistaken....

CAPTAIN LEWIS, Drouillard, and several Shoshones sat in a circle outside Cameahwait's brush lodge. The chief told them that they would not be able to take the Jefferson River through the mountains. That in fact there was no floatable river through the mountains. He drew a map in the dust with a stick, piling up mounds of dirt to depict the terrible mountains. He explained that his tribe had never been on the other side of the mountains because the journey was too dangerous.

"He must be mistaken," the Captain said to Drouillard.

"I don't think so, Captain. His people have been living here for a long time."

Captain Lewis stared at the shells tied into Drouillard's bushy hair, then pulled off one of the shells in his own hair and held it out to Cameahwait. "Ask him where he got this seashell."

Drouillard made the signs and Cameahwait nodded and gave a long discourse in hand-talk.

"He says that the shells came from the Nez Percé tribe on the west side of the mountains," Drouillard explained. "They get them from Indians downriver, who get them from Indians farther downriver. The Nez Percé and Flathead tribes come over to this side of the mountains to hunt buffalo and to trade. They also come over to fight the Blackfeet Indians, who steal from them and take their women and are very bad people."

We had heard this about the Blackfeet from every tribe we had talked with. It was said that they had gotten muskets from the French trading post to the north and that they knew how to use them.

"If Nez Percé and Flatheads can cross the mountains," the Captain said, "we can cross the mountains. The chief must be exaggerating the difficulties."

"Why would he do that?" Drouillard asked.

"In order to keep us here with our rifles. These people are starving. Our guns could help get meat for them."

"Providing there's meat around here," Drouillard said, "which I have not seen hide nor hair of. No, I think the chief is telling us the truth about the mountains."

If Cameahwait was right, then there was no Northwest Passage. Captain Lewis could not quite get his mind around what he had just heard. I had spent many nights listening to the captains discuss this passage and what it meant to the future of their country. It was a severe blow for him. He sat mute for several minutes, staring at the mounds of dirt.

Cameahwait became increasingly uncomfortable with the silence. "I have upset your chief," he signed, looking concerned.

Drouillard shook his head. "He is just admiring your fine map." He nudged Captain Lewis. "Captain?"

Captain Lewis looked up.

"We need to continue the parley," Drouillard said quietly.

"Yes, of course." The Captain smiled at Cameahwait, but there was no real joy behind it. "Ask him if there is anyone who has been over the mountains who could speak to us about the route."

Cameahwait talked with the other Shoshones sitting with us, then told us there was one man who had made the journey many years ago.

"Can we talk to him?"

Cameahwait said the man lived in another encampment a few miles away, but he would be happy to take us to him.

A large number of Shoshones followed us as we walked across the prairie, laughing and chattering away. The Shoshones were a handsome people, although somewhat gaunt from lack of food. Their clothing was made out of beautifully tanned deerskin decorated with beads and shells. Some of the men wore a fur garment draped over their shoulders, called a tippet, made of river otter or delicate ermine skins. Others wore robes made from prairie wolf, antelope, deer, or buffalo skins. Like other tribes we had encountered, most of the men wore scalps taken from their enemies tied to their leggings.

I liked these Shoshones. They were very outgoing and friendly. The same could not be said for their dogs, who were the snappiest mongrels I had yet encountered along the trail. The only things that kept them at bay were my size and the occasional kick and whack from the Shoshones, who considered it rude for them to bite at me.

The Captain named the old man who had been across the mountains Old Toby, because the Captain couldn't pronounce his real name. We sat outside Old Toby's lodge and Captain Lewis shared a pipe of our tobacco with him.

Old Toby told the Captain that the mountains were very perilous this time of year.

"No food," he signed. "Horses fall from cliffs. Men will be crippled with foot soreness. The snow will freeze all of you to death."

Captain Lewis was undeterred. "Ask him if there is a big river going through the mountains." His mind was still on the Northwest Passage.

"There are no rivers you can take to get through the mountains, but there is a big river on the other side that leads to a stinking lake with water you cannot drink."

"The Pacific. The big river must be the Columbia."

The Captain and Drouillard spent the rest of the afternoon talking to Old Toby and Cameahwait. The chief readily agreed to lend us thirty horses to retrieve our supplies at the Jefferson River, and consented to lead us there and lend a hand.

Captain Lewis asked Old Toby if he would guide us over the mountains. Old Toby said he would think about it and let us know in a few days.

That night in camp there was a lot of talk among the Shoshones about the wisdom of taking us to the

Jefferson. Most of them believed we were leading them into a trap and would kill them. By morning they were convinced of this and Cameahwait informed Captain Lewis that he was still willing to take us but his men refused to go.

Captain Lewis began haranguing the Shoshone men, with Drouillard translating his harsh words into hand-talk. The Captain called them cowards, challenged their manhood, and said other rough things, which Drouillard had a difficult time expressing.

Cameahwait joined the Captain in the harangue. He swung onto his horse and yelled that he would rather die than break his word to the Captain. And if the Captain planned on killing him, he was not afraid to die. He had to repeat this speech three times before a few of his men were shamed enough to mount their horses. When we left the village there was much crying and wailing. The women were convinced the men were riding off to certain death.

Not long after we left we were joined by a dozen more men. A little later it seemed as if the entire village had joined us—men, women, children, and dogs were strung out for a mile behind us. I suspected their change of heart was brought on not by courage but by their empty bellies. They did not want to miss the chance that our rifles might get lucky.

That night the Captain sent Drouillard ahead to hunt, but he returned a few hours later without anything. Captain Lewis mixed the last of the flour and divided it. He gave me half of his portion, but it was like dropping a pebble into a dry well. I was almost ready to eat some dirt, just for the pleasure of having something inside of me.

Early the following morning Captain Lewis again sent Drouillard out ahead to hunt. I wanted to go with him, but the Captain wouldn't allow it.

"You stick around, Sea. I don't want you chasing the game off."

A ridiculous notion, but I had no choice in the matter. We waited before proceeding, to give Drouillard a head start.

We hadn't gone far when a Shoshone who had been following Drouillard came galloping up, screaming that Drouillard had shot a deer. The Shoshones ran in the direction the rider had come from, like the prairie was on fire behind them. Captain Lewis and I followed at a more dignified pace, although I wanted to bolt ahead.

When we arrived, there was a scene I would not have believed if I hadn't seen it with my own eyes. Drouillard had stripped the guts out of the deer and the Shoshones were at the pile like a pack of famished wolves. Blood dribbled out of the corners of their mouths as they gulped down pieces of heart, lungs, and liver. One of the braves had gotten ahold of a string of intestine and was feeding it into his mouth with one hand as he pushed the foul contents out with the other hand. They were eating *my* food! I was about to join the fray, but Captain Lewis stopped me.

"Steady, Sea…Better wait for them to get their bellies full or they're liable to gobble you down right along with the deer."

"*Caw! Caw! Caw!*"

White Feather appeared in the tree above the Indians. I barked a greeting up to him.

"Quiet, Sea!" Captain Lewis scolded. "You'll get your turn."

The crow flew down to the ground and landed right in front of me. He allowed me to sniff him but to my surprise I could not pick up a single scent from his shiny feathers. I glanced at Captain Lewis and when I looked back, White Feather was gone.

"I'll go off and see if I can get another deer," Drouillard said.

McNeal had managed to save a quarter of the deer for us. We stood guard over our small pile of meat and watched the Shoshones devour every remaining scrap of flesh, including the soft part of the deer's hooves. When they finished the meat, they gnawed the bones clean, bit knuckles off the ends, and sucked the bones hollow.

We heard the report of Drouillard's rifle. The Shoshones ran to the sound, and the scene was repeated.

A short time later Drouillard fired again at some distance, but the Shoshones stayed put. He walked up with a third deer slung over his shoulder. The Shoshones didn't even get up. I was reminded of the wolves we had seen along the Missouri too gorged with meat to move.

"Looks like our guests are full," the Captain said. He began building a fire to cook our dinner. I couldn't wait and started in on the deer entrails, joined by a half dozen ravenous Shoshone dogs.

When we finished eating, our large party proceeded over to the Jefferson. As we approached the river the Shoshones once again grew suspicious that we were leading them into a trap. They began talking of returning to their village, and one shouted that the white men had filled their bellies with meat to dull them.

Chief Cameahwait began taking the fur tippets from around his men's necks and putting them on our men. "If we are attacked," he said, "they will not be able to tell the difference between their tribe and ours."

Captain Lewis, desperate to keep the Shoshones at the river, took the deception a step further by putting his cocked hat on Cameahwait's head. The other men followed suit and gave their hats to the Shoshones.

The Captain turned to Drouillard. "Tell Cameahwait that our other chief will be waiting for us at the fork when we arrive."

But when the fork came into view, Captain Clark was not there. Near the fork was a thick stand of trees that could easily conceal a whole tribe of warriors. This started another round of fear and suspicion. Cameahwait balked and brought the party to a halt.

Fearing the Shoshones were about to turn their horses around, Captain Lewis handed his rifle to Cameahwait. Turning to Drouillard Lewis said, "Tell him that if his enemies are in those trees, he can defend himself with my rifle."

At first Drouillard was too shocked to raise his hands. He stared at the Captain with his mouth open.

"Tell him!"

Drouillard reluctantly made the signs.

Cameahwait understood, but he still hesitated to move forward.

"Tell him that I am not afraid to die," Captain Lewis said. "Tell him that if I have deceived him he can shoot me."

"I don't think that's—," Drouillard began.

"Tell him!"

Drouillard did as he was ordered.

"Now give your rifles to the Shoshones."

Drouillard, McNeal, and Shields looked as if they thought the Captain had lost his mind. The men didn't like having their best friends hold their rifles, and now the Captain was asking them to give them up to complete strangers. And Indians to boot.

"Do it now!"

I think this was the hardest thing these men had ever done, but each of them handed his rifle to the Shoshone next to him. This bold gesture seemed to calm Cameahwait and his men down somewhat, and we proceeded on to the fork.

When we got there, Captain Lewis asked Drouillard in a rather loud cheerful voice if he remembered the place where we had left the note for Captain Clark downriver. We had put the note there several days earlier to apprise him of our situation.

"Yes, sir."

"Good! Take one of the Indians to the river and bring the note back to me."

"But *you* wrote—"

"Act like you've never seen the note before and make sure your friend sees you *find* it."

Drouillard nodded and returned awhile later with the note, trying to act very excited, which was not an easy role for him to play. Captain Lewis grabbed the note out of his hand as if Drouillard had brought him a sack of gold. He showed it to Chief Cameahwait, claiming it was from Captain Clark informing them that Clark and his men would be along the following day and to wait there for them. Cameahwait looked the note over carefully and seemed fascinated with the idea that the captains could communicate with each other by making little marks on paper.

"What will we do if Captain Clark doesn't arrive at the fork tomorrow?" McNeal asked.

"I have no idea," Captain Lewis said.

That night, for the benefit of the Shoshones, the Captain feigned a jovial confidence he did not feel. The Captain's cheerfulness seemed strained. The Shoshones were not fooled. They knew something was wrong. When the Captain unrolled his blanket for the night near the fire, they put their beds all around him so he could not leave.

August 17, 1805
I slept very little last night, worrying about what I will do if Captain Clark does not arrive today. What could be keeping him? Any number of things, I realize. It is so frustrating to wait here knowing that with each passing minute the Shoshones may bolt like frightened deer. They have been raided so many times in recent years, they trust no one. I cannot blame them. According to Cameahwait, their numbers have been greatly reduced from disease and starvation as well as war. They have been left with barely enough men of fighting age to defend themselves.

I sent Drouillard downriver with an Indian, hoping he can intercept Captain Clark and hurry him along....

"There's ink spilled over this page," Colter says. "Pass me that canteen."

Drouillard hands it over.

CAPTAIN LEWIS spilled the ink when the brave who had accompanied Drouillard came running into camp yelling that there were white men in boats coming up-river.

Captain Lewis jumped to his feet. He didn't notice the ink he spilled because Chief Cameahwait had him in a bear hug. Though Captain Lewis hadn't understood the brave's words, he understood Cameahwait's enthusiasm and it was hard to say which of them was more excited. Captain Lewis could now get his horses and perhaps get through the mountains before winter set in. But Cameahwait had even more at stake. The arrival of Captain Clark meant he had not led his people into an ambush.

A few minutes later Captain Clark, Charbonneau, Bird Woman, and Drouillard walked into camp ahead of the men in the canoes. The Shoshones swarmed to Captain Clark. When Chief Cameahwait finished hugging him, the chief tied a bunch of seashells in Captain Clark's hair. Then Captain Lewis was finally able to cut through the crowd and reach his friend. The two men embraced and there were tears in the eyes of both.

I stood off to the side to save my paws from getting tromped upon. Bird Woman saw me and reached into her pouch for a dead mouse, which I swallowed in one gulp. She hunched down and turned so I could see Pomp. He seemed to have grown a great deal during our short separation. Bird Woman was going to have to make a bigger cradleboard to accommodate him soon. He grinned and laughed, and I gave him a wet lick across his brown face. I was about to give him another for good measure when Bird Woman squealed in delight, running toward a young Shoshone woman about her age. The women hugged and cried and laughed and cried and chattered in rapid Shoshone. I was able to understand enough of their conversation to learn that this was Bird Woman's friend Jumping Fish, the girl who had gotten away the day Bird Woman was captured by the Hidatsas.

The other Shoshones were too busy with Captain Clark to notice this reunion. Jumping Fish led Bird Woman away from the crowd. They took Pomp out of the cradleboard and while they talked, I played with him. I was surprised at how much I had missed him. I let him pull my fur and crawl around after me.

As we were playing, Charbonneau walked up and told Bird Woman that he had been looking for her. "We're ready to parley and we need you to speak Shoshone for us."

"We will talk again when I finish," Bird Woman said to Jumping Fish. "Will you watch my son while I'm gone?"

Everyone was already gathered beneath the awning when Bird Woman arrived with Charbonneau. The large circle of men stopped talking as she approached and sat down next to her husband with her head lowered. Captain Lewis explained that the words would flow from him in English to Labiche, from Labiche to Charbonneau in French, from Charbonneau to Bird Woman in Hidatsa, and from Bird Woman to the chief in Shoshone.

Bird Woman looked up and saw Cameahwait for the first time. Her eyes got wide and she yelled out, *"Ah-ah-hi! Ah-ah-hi!"* She jumped to her feet and rushed toward the chief. The captains stared at her in complete shock. Before they could stop her, she was in Cameahwait's arms.

For the next few minutes there was a great deal of confusion. Cameahwait and Bird Woman were hugging and crying, and the other Shoshones were on their feet jumping up and down as if they were standing on hot coals.

"What the devil is going on, Mister Charbonneau?" Captain Lewis asked, irritated that the dignity of his parley had been shattered.

"Well..." Charbonneau struggled to explain. "Well...it seems—"

"Spit it out, man!"

"Chief Cameahwait is my wife's brother!"

"I thought he had been killed in the Hidatsa raid."

"Apparently not," Captain Clark said, grinning.

"And if Cameahwait had any suspicion about our sincerity, this will certainly put an end to it."

Cameahwait continued hugging his sister. Tears flowed down his face and several of the Shoshones were now crying along with him.

After a time things settled down enough for the parley to begin, and they talked until after dark. Every once in a while Bird Woman would be overwhelmed with emotion and begin weeping, but she managed her part of the translation. Cameahwait promised to provide the party with as many horses as they needed. He also said that he would lead us to the trail the Indians used to cross the mountains.

August 18, 1805
Captain Clark rode off this morning with 11 men to scout
the river and determine if we can ascend it with our canoes.
From what we've heard, this now seems doubtful. The rest of
the men are in camp with me, making saddles for the horses
and preparing for our push over the mountains.

Cameahwait has promised to take us to the mountains,
but not over them, as he has not been that way himself and
he must head to the buffalo grounds soon to gather meat for
the winter.

Today is my 31st birthday. I fear I have done little with
my life to further the happiness of the human race. I view
with regret the hours I have spent in indolence, and now wish
I had those hours back to spend more wisely. I will endeavor
to do better....

Colter shakes his head. "Now, isn't that just like
the Captain? He's led us nearly all the way across
the country, discovered dozens of new animals and

plants, made friends with hundreds of Indians, and in the process lost only one man. And he thinks he hasn't done anything with his life?"

"It's a puzzlement, all right," Drouillard says. "But I guess that's just the way Captain Lewis is. What's he have to say next?"

August 29, 1805
We are ready for the mountains. We have 29 horses and the word of Old Toby that he will guide us.

The possibility of a Northwest Passage seems to have come to an end with the tremendous mountains we must cross. Captain Clark has returned with the belief that there are no navigable rivers through the mountains, so the primary objective of our journey cannot be fulfilled. This is not a failure on our part, but I am very disappointed, considering the hardships we have endured searching for something that does not exist.

Surprisingly, the men seem little bothered by this. Even Captain Clark does not seem overly concerned. His only comment was, "We have solved a 300-year-old mystery. The answer is, there is no Northwest Passage." He laughed heartily, as if this were the funniest irony he had ever heard.

The only thing that keeps me going and dulls the pain of this disappointment is my concern for the men. I pray the mountains will not take any of them and that there is ample food on the other side.

Old Toby is a frail old man, and I fear that he is not

strong enough for a journey such as this. Fortunately his two sons are with him....

BENEATH OLD TOBY'S loose wrinkled skin was a core of iron that eventually put all the men to shame, but Captain Lewis was right to worry about our crossing.

The trails through the foothills leading to the mountains were steep and slippery. There was little food. Horses fell and tumbled down deep ravines. In our first few days we lost two horses from exhaustion and another was crippled and had to be shot.

When Old Toby's sons left to rejoin the Shoshones to hunt buffalo, Captain Lewis nearly begged them to stay.

"We cannot," one of them responded through Bird Woman. "We must help with the buffalo."

"You can return as soon as we get to the other side of the mountains."

"Winter may stop them from returning," Old Toby said. "What then?"

"We will pay them generously."

Old Toby shook his head. "My sons and their families cannot eat your gifts. I am too old to hunt. I will not be missed. I will take you over the mountains alone."

September 3, 1805
Two inches of snow on the ground. Sleet falling. Captain
Clark shot four pheasants, which we divided among our-
selves, along with some corn. Our guide eats virtually noth-
ing. I caught him sharing his portion with my dog....

Colter shakes his head. "That Toby was one tough
old cuss."

"He was that."

THAT TOUGH OLD CUSS saved me from starving. A few
handfuls of bird guts would not have gotten me far.

When we moved from the foothills into the mountains, we met up with a group of Flathead Indians who
were on their way to join the Shoshones to hunt buffalo.
Their chief was named Three Eagles.

"We have been watching your tribe for the past several days," he explained in hand-talk. He pointed to

York. "I thought this man was painted with black paint because you were going to war. But by the casual way your tribe was riding and the fact that you had a woman and child with you, I knew you were not a raiding party. So I decided to greet you as friends."

I'm not sure the captains understood how fortunate we were. Three Eagles had eighty warriors in his camp and could have easily overwhelmed us. Instead they fed us from their meager supply of food and shared information with the captains about what lay on the west side of the mountains.

Captain Lewis tried to trade for food, but Three Eagles's people had none to spare. They did have extra horses, though, and we'd ended up with several of them by the time the Flatheads proceeded downhill and we proceeded up.

That evening the hunters killed only two small birds, which we made into a stew with corn. Divided between so many, the meal was hardly worth the bother of cooking. Once again Old Toby shared his small portion with me.

Each day we encountered steeper terrain, narrower trails, and dropping temperatures. Food became a distant memory.

September 7, 1805
Raining. Cold.

September 9, 1805
*Arrived at a stream we are calling Traveler's Rest because
that is what we intend to do. Drouillard killed a deer, and
another man an elk.*

September 10, 1805
Sent the men out hunting. Snow on the ground. Very cold.

Colter looks at Mountain Dog and grins. "This
was about the time I first laid eyes on you,
Mountain Dog," he signs. " 'Course you were just a
boy then. You've filled out a mite over the years."

Mountain Dog smiles back. "I ran away from
you," he signs.

"Like a jackrabbit."

I was with Colter. We were hunting, but most of

the animals had moved down to the plains for the winter, so we were not having any luck.

I SAW WHITE FEATHER flying through the trees and I barked at him. Colter got excited. "What is it? You on to something, Sea? Let's go get it, boy!"

White Feather led us up a steep hill. Halfway to the top I picked up human scent. Not fresh, but not too old, either.

Colter sensed my interest. "You're on to it now, Sea," he said breathlessly. "Let's get that cuss!"

I hurried ahead. On top of the ridge was a pile of huge round boulders. Sitting cross-legged on the highest boulder was a young boy, maybe fourteen or fifteen years old. And except for the buffalo robe under his bottom, he was stark naked.

The wind was howling up on that ridge, snow blowing everywhere, but that boy looked as cozy as a pup suckling his mother. He had his eyes closed and was quietly singing something in a tongue I had never heard. White Feather was standing right in front of him. I sat below the boulder looking up at them, somehow knowing I had stumbled across something I wasn't supposed to disturb.

Colter slipped on an icy spot just as he topped the ridge, and let out a yell. The boy's head snapped up and his eyes locked on mine for a second or two and he smiled. But the smile disappeared when he saw Colter coming up behind me.

"What the devil?" Colter said. "I'll be a—"

The boy and the robe were up and gone before Colter could describe what he would be.

We searched for a good hour, but other than the boy's footprints in the snow we could find neither hide nor hair of him.

The boy was not the only Indian we saw that day. On our way back we came across three mounted Indians who seemed even less pleased to see us than the boy had been. Their faces were as taut as their bowstrings—all three of which were pointed right at Colter's heart.

"Flatheads," Colter said.

But I could tell they were from a different tribe altogether.

"Now, don't get riled," Colter said, and gave them his most charming grin, which had absolutely no effect on them. Their forearms began to tremble from the strain of the loaded bows. Colter laid his rifle on the ground. The Indians relaxed their pull but kept their arrows notched.

With very poor hand-talk Colter attempted to explain who he was and what he was doing on the mountain. The Indians didn't catch all of his meaning, but they understood enough to agree to follow us back to Traveler's Rest.

The captains smoked the pipe with the Indians and

learned they were from the Nez Percé tribe, or the Nee-mee-poo as they call themselves, meaning "the people." The Nez Percé explained to the captains they were after a band of Shoshones who had stolen twenty-three of their best horses from their village on the west side of the mountain. Captain Lewis fed them, then asked if they would lead us to their village. He was still doubtful that Old Toby was up to the task.

The Nez Percé braves discussed the possibility among themselves, then signed to Drouillard that they had to pursue the thieves who stole their horses and they could not delay.

"Sorry, Captain," Drouillard said.

"We have to convince at least one of them to take us over, Drouillard! I don't think that Old Toby is up to the task. Ask them again. Tell them we'll give them gifts when we reach their land safely."

Drouillard tried again. Finally one of the braves said he would guide us, but he seemed to agree more out of politeness than desire.

September 11, 1805
No meat taken today. The Nez Percé who agreed yesterday
to guide us over the mountains was gone this morning and
has not returned, so we are still relying on Old Toby to take
us across....

I WAS NOT SURPRISED the brave had a change of heart. After his friends left he sat around camp looking forlorn and confused. I saw him get up in the middle of the night, load his horse, and leave, making no more noise than a mouse walking on damp moss. I let out a couple of barks when he left, but the men were too cold to crawl out from beneath their blankets and look.

The next day the most difficult part of our journey began. The hillsides were covered with downed trees, snow, and slick ice. I was as cold as I had ever been in my life. The frigid air burned my eyes, the ice froze on my muzzle, and the snow balled up between my toes, making each step a painful ordeal. As cold and miserable as I was, it was nothing compared to what the men endured. Swathed in blankets and furs, they plodded ahead in hungry silence, knowing if they stopped moving the cold would consume them. On the narrower ledges the men had to get off and lead their terrified mounts across, but the horses still slipped and fell, sometimes all the way to the bottom of the hill. Wearily, the men followed the horses down, picking up spilled gear on the way, catching and repacking the animals, then starting back up again from where they had started. The delays caused the party to string out along the trail for miles. Some of the men didn't arrive in camp until well after dark, when they found the men who had gotten there earlier fast asleep.

September 13, 1805
A few of our horses strayed this morning, causing further
delays. Four grouse and one poor deer for dinner. Camped
at a hot springs....

I STAYED IN FRONT of the fray with Old Toby—out of
range of the men's foul tempers, which were not improved by their empty bellies. We were the first to arrive
at the hot springs, which were something I had never
seen before. At first I mistook the steam rising in the
cold air for smoke and thought the pools were on fire. I
barked in alarm. Old Toby smiled at my apprehension,
then took his clothes off, and to my surprise sat down in
one of the pools with a satisfied sigh.

While he bathed I dug around the old campfires
and found some bones to chew. When I had harvested
everything I could find I joined Old Toby in the pool,

and that's when the first men stumbled into camp and found us. They were too tired to take their clothes off and partake of the soothing water, but a few of them managed the strength to shed their moccasins and soak their swollen feet.

September 14, 1805
Rain, hail. Horses and men very fatigued. Killed a colt to
eat.

September 15, 1805
Old Toby got us lost.

September 16, 1805
Eight inches of snow on the ground, making it very difficult
to follow the trail. There is no water up here so at night we
boil snow over the fires. Killed our second colt....

OLD TOBY ONLY made that one mistake in all our time in the mountains. He hadn't been over the mountains in ten years, and he got a little confused by the fallen trees and snow on the ground.

He didn't discover his mistake until we had gone four miles, and compensated for it by leading us up an incredibly steep, tree-strewn hillside to the top of a high ridge, with the men grumbling all the way.

"Looks different now," was his only comment when Captain Lewis asked him why he had led us astray.

The next afternoon I joined Captain Clark and Colter as they forged ahead of the main party to find a good campsite and start the fires. As they brushed against the trees on the narrow trail, small icy avalanches tumbled onto their heads and down the necks of their shirts. By the time we found a likely site both men were nearly frozen. It was a wonder they could get the fires started with their numb hands.

"We have to get off this mountain," Captain Clark said through chattering teeth.

A few hours later the men began to straggle in, looking as grim and haggard as I had ever seen them. They squatted around the fires in wooden silence, watching steam rise from each other's buckskins.

Captain Clark killed the second colt and started the red flesh roasting.

The next day and night were much the same. The men grew weaker with every passing hour. The horses' legs trembled from lack of food, from strain, and from terror at the dizzying heights along the narrow slippery trails. Several fell, smashing the fragile loads as they tumbled down the steep embankments. The men killed the last colt.

"We can't continue like this," Captain Clark said. "We'll never make it to the other side."

Captain Lewis looked around the camp at the men and nodded. "What do you suggest?"

"I don't like to split up, but I think one of us should go ahead with our best hunters. Try to reach the west side, where there must be more game, or at least Indians we can buy food from."

Captain Lewis nodded wearily. "I'll stay back."

"We'll travel light. I'll try to get food back up to you as soon as I can."

The Captain looked at the men again. "You had better, old friend, or we won't need it."

September 18, 1805
Captain Clark has gone ahead. No food. Our spirits very low.

I KNEW THAT IF I didn't get some food soon I wouldn't have the strength to get through the mountains. I joined Captain Clark and the hunters. We made a forced march of more than thirty miles, up and down the difficult terrain. At the end of that terrible day we were rewarded with a view far below us of an immense green plateau.

"We should reach it by tomorrow," Captain Clark predicted.

Early the following morning we proceeded on. Reubin Fields caught a horse in a glade and brought it to Captain Clark.

"Shoot it," Captain Clark ordered. "We'll eat some and leave the rest for Captain Lewis and the others."

The next day we reached the plain and came upon three young Nez Percé boys playing with toy bows. As soon as they saw us they ran like antelope and hid themselves, but I found the frightened boys easily in the tall grass.

Captain Clark gave them some trinkets, which helped soothe their nerves. They led us to their village with their shoulders thrown back and their bony chests stuck out, like the proud warriors they would one day become.

The camp was filled with women, children, and old men. They explained through hand-talk that their men were away on a raiding party, but they expected them back soon.

Captain Clark asked for food and we were given baskets of camas root—a bulblike plant the men found delicious. I was famished but could not make myself eat the plant. I started sniffing around for something else to fill my belly.

A couple of Indian dogs followed me as I rambled through the village, but they kept their distance because I was considerably bigger than they were, despite having lost some of my bulk crossing the mountains.

The Nez Percé lodges were made of poles overlaid with bark mats. Outside the lodges were piles of camas and other roots, and I reckoned we were in a temporary camp set up to gather these roots in the nearby meadows.

"You," someone called in French, "big dog…"

I was surprised to hear this language. The Nez Percé who greeted us had said we were the first white men they had laid eyes on.

"Over here…"

The words came from a very old woman sitting on a log outside a lodge. I walked over to her.

"I have heard of you, big dog," she said.

I was pondering how this could be when a teenage boy stepped out of her lodge into the bright sun rubbing his eyes. He looked a bit different with clothes on, but there was no mistaking him—it was the same boy Colter and I had discovered up on the mountain. When the boy saw me, he started jumping up and down, screaming and pointing at me. His wild gesticulating frightened me, and I was on the verge of running off, but he beat me to it, disappearing behind the lodge as fast as he had on the day we first saw him.

The old woman started laughing. When she stopped she said, "The others said my grandson couldn't have seen a big black dog during his quest for his *wyakin*. They said he must have seen a wolf, but you look more like a bear to me. I will call you Yahka—Black Bear.

"By showing yourself here, you have made my grandson very happy. For that you deserve some salmon. Come with me, Yahka."

I had not heard the word *salmon* before, but I hoped

it meant food. The word *wyakin* was also new. I learned later it meant "spirit guide." When the Nez Percé reach a certain age they go to a sacred place to fast and pray until they are visited by an animal spirit who will guide them throughout their lives.

I followed the old woman over to a long scaffold made of sticks. Hanging on the sticks were dozens of colossal fish, split in two lengthwise, drying in the sun. She threw one down on the ground in front of me.

"Eat."

I was not fond of fish, but my hunger drove me to try the orange flesh. To my relief it had a different taste than the fish I had eaten previously, but was a far cry from buffalo, deer, and elk flesh.

"You had better get used to salmon," she said. "It is all you will be eating for a long time."

I did get used to it. But my taste for it was not shared by our tribe, which was a shame, as there was enough of this fish drying on the scaffolds in this one camp to feed them for several months.

Halfway through my salmon the boy returned with an old man and a group of boys, pointing at me and shouting excitedly as he approached. The old man grinned as he watched me eat, then said something to the boy.

From that day on they called the boy Mountain Dog. He and I were to become very good friends.

September 20, 1805
Today we found the remains of a horse Captain Clark left
us. It was very agreeable....

"More agreeable than what we had, I reckon,"
Colter says.

Drouillard shakes his head. "It's a wonder none
of us died from that root."

THE MEN HAD GOTTEN very sick from eating too much
camas. The following morning some of them had so
much pain in their bellies they could not stand up.
Captain Clark sent those who could walk out hunting,
except for Reubin Fields. He was sent back toward the
mountains to find Captain Lewis with a load of dried
salmon and camas root the Nez Percé provided.

"Make sure you tell them to go easy on that root,"
Captain Clark said.

"Yes, sir," Reubin said.

While the men were out hunting Captain Clark rambled over to another camp along the river where it was said their chief, a man named Twisted Hair, was fishing.

I did not go with Captain Clark, nor did I join Reubin or the men hunting. Instead I stayed in camp with Mountain Dog, following him around as he proudly showed me off to his friends. I had never been around a young boy and found it very much to my liking. He and his friends were filled with enormous energy and a boundless sense of fun. They were constantly laughing, racing their horses, and playing jokes on one another. It brought to mind the fun we'd had before we started up the Missouri.

Mountain Dog lived with three other boys his age in a lodge not far from his grandmother, whose name I learned was Watkuweis, which meant "returned from a faraway country." That night I learned how she had gotten this name.

Mountain Dog and his friends were gathered around Watkuweis's fire exchanging stories. When they had exhausted their supply, one of the boys asked Watkuweis to tell her story.

"But you know my story," she said.

"Please."

Watkuweis looked deep into the fire and began....

"When I was a young girl I traveled east of the

mountains with my family to hunt the buffalo. We had been there for some time gathering and preparing the meat and the skins, and we were ready to come home. But on the day we were to leave, the Blackfeet fell upon us. They killed everyone in my family and took me with them.

"I lived as a slave in their village for a long and terrible time. The Blackfeet are as cruel as every story you have heard about them. The only thing that kept me alive was the thought that I would one day escape and return here.

"After a time the man who owned me took me north for many days. We arrived at a huge lodge made of trees stacked together, higher than one can climb. The lodge was called a fort. The men who lived inside had white skin, and hair on their faces and chests, like the men who have come to visit us here. They trapped and traded for furs, and their ways were very different from ours.

"The Blackfeet who owned me traded me to a white man for a musket. At first I was very frightened, but the white man who bought me was a good man. He treated me well. We lived together for many years and I bore him a son, but still I dreamed of returning home.

"When our son was still small, I was told by a white woman living at the fort that the men were going back to their home across the big water. 'They are never coming back,' she said. 'And they are taking you with them.'

"Of all the bad things that had happened to me, this would have been the most terrible, because it would have meant I could never see my home again. The white woman helped me to escape. She gave me a hatchet and some food. One night as the men slept I put my son in a cradleboard and left the fort.

"I went east toward the mountains. Suns and storms beat me down. Wild animals chased me. Streams and rivers barred my way. I was constantly afraid the Blackfeet would find me. But I continued on.

"Whenever I was too afraid to take another step, my *wyakin*—a great wolf—encouraged me to continue and told me which way to go.

"I made a raft to cross a big river. As I crossed, a bear attacked me but I killed him with my hatchet.

"My baby began to weaken because we had no food. I found a pile of old bones that still had some meat on them. I cooked this meat and fed some to my baby, but the meat was bad. My baby died. I dug a shallow grave with my hands and buried him.

"When I finally reached the mountains my strength left me. I lay there for many days waiting for death, but instead a group of Nee-mee-poo hunters found me and took me across the mountains to my home."

September 22, 1805
Private R. Fields found us today and brought camas root
and salmon. These mountains will soon be behind us....

Colter stands and stretches. "We're getting toward
the end, but I've had about enough for tonight."

"What do you mean, we're toward the end?"
Drouillard asks in surprise.

"The end of the red book. The Captain doesn't
make another entry until January 1, 1806, when we
were at Fort Clatsop."

Drouillard takes the book and flips through the
few remaining pages. "Guess we can finish it up
tomorrow, then." He explains this to Watkuweis.

Mountain Dog puts the red book into the
pouch, and he and Watkuweis walk back to their
tepee.

Colter rolls his blanket out next to the fire.
"They got most of them buffalo hides cleaned up

this afternoon. I suspect they'll be moving on soon. You think Twisted Hair will be back tomorrow?"

"Or the next day," Drouillard says. "Funny the Captain didn't write much after we got over them mountains."

"He wasn't the same after that."

The evening is warm and clear and windy. I feel restless and ramble out onto the prairie, where the yellow moon is so bright the buffalo cast shadows on the ground. I think about Captain Lewis and the men during that final year. Colter is right, the Captain was not the same after crossing the mountains—but neither were the other men, and neither was I.

I find a sheltered place among some rocks and lie down. A great deal happened during the months the Captain chose not to write in the red book. I close my eyes and remember....

WHEN CAPTAIN LEWIS and the other men arrived at the camas camp they looked more dead than alive—cheeks sunken, buckskins filthy and torn, moccasins shredded—and they barely had the strength to pull the packs off their thin horses.

The Captain lay down outside a lodge, clutched his knees, and began to moan. He wasn't alone.

"I told them to take it easy on that camas and fish,"

Reubin said. "But they were so hungry they couldn't help themselves."

Bird Woman, Pomp, and Old Toby were not afflicted. In fact when Bird Woman saw me she smiled broadly, scratched my ears, then reached into her pouch and gave me a dead mouse.

The Nez Percé gathered around as the men unloaded the horses. They were astonished at the collection of goods, but what impressed them most were the rifles.

That night the Nez Percé men met at the lodge next door to Watkuweis's. They talked for hours about our tribe and our goods.

"If we had those rifles we could protect ourselves from our enemies."

"We could kill deer and elk in the winter when the salmon is gone."

"Did you see the metal tomahawk for cutting trees? With that we could build shelters and cut wood for our fires in no time at all."

Watkuweis sat outside her lodge pounding camas root on a flat stone, listening to their conversation.

"The white men are very sick," one of the men said.

"Even their chiefs are weakened," another added.

"It would be easy to have these things for ourselves."

Watkuweis got up and walked over to them.

"I hear your talk," she said. "The white men were very good to me even though I was a stranger to them."

"We are just talking, Watkuweis. There is no harm in talk."

"Bad talk leads to bad actions. You talk like the Blackfeet."

The men stared at the fire, chastened.

"These men have done nothing to you," she said. "Do them no harm!"

And they didn't. Instead they were very kind to our tribe. We moved our camp to the Clearwater River. Captain Clark had the men who felt well enough cut trees for dugout canoes. The Nez Percé showed them an easier way to hollow out the logs by using hot coals from the fire. Chief Twisted Hair said he would care for our horses and saddles while we were gone in exchange for two rifles. He helped us brand the horses so we would know which ones were ours when we returned. Every day people from different villages came to camp with food to sell. In the evenings Captain Clark treated the Nez Percé ills in exchange for horses and other items.

We stayed with the Nez Percé for several weeks, preparing for the last leg of our journey to the Pacific Ocean.

During most of that time Captain Lewis was so sick he could not sit up. I stayed with him most nights, but during the day I spent my time with Mountain Dog and his friends, who had built a shelter close to the canoe camp so they would not miss any of the excitement of having us there.

They took me hunting with bows and arrows, although we rarely saw any game. Hunting was just an excuse to get on horseback and race each other to the tops of hills. They took me upriver, where they speared salmon, which were more numerous than the buffalo east of the mountains. In some spots the fish were so thick you could have crossed the river on their fins. They took me up into the mountains, a place Mountain Dog knew very well, and with him I lost my fear of the mountains' bite. And there I discovered something.

Mountain Dog and his friends were on foot tracking a deer up a draw when I heard *"Caw! Caw! Caw!"* I had not seen White Feather since Traveler's Rest. He was perched in a lightning-struck tree. I stopped and barked.

"He's scaring the deer!"

Mountain Dog ignored his friend's complaint and looked up at the tree. "What's he looking at?" he asked.

I stared at Mountain Dog. Surely he and his friends could see and hear White Feather.

"Perhaps he sees his spirit guide," one of his friends said, laughing.

"A dog with a spirit guide?" the other scoffed.

"Caw! Caw! Caw!"

I was bewildered. How could they not see and hear White Feather? Mountain Dog and his friends continued up the draw after the deer, but I stayed below the tree staring up at my companion, trying to make sense of what had just occurred. I thought back to all the other times White Feather had appeared, trying to remember if my human companions had ever acknowledged his presence. If they had, I didn't recall it. It would be some time before I discovered what this meant.

The men began complaining about having nothing to eat except salmon and camas roots. They killed a horse to eat, but this did not slake their appetite. One day as I returned to camp from a ramble upriver with Mountain Dog, I smelled meat roasting, but it was not horse or any other animal flesh I had smelled before. I hurried along and when I got there, I found the men standing around the fires pushing meat into their mouths. Captain Lewis was with them, and so was Bird Woman. She had Pomp in her lap and was feeding him little pieces she had pulled off a bone.

"I believe this is the most delicious meat I've ever

eaten," the Captain said between mouthfuls. "It is far superior to either deer or elk, and it is certainly better than horse."

Several Nez Percé stood off to the side. They were trying to hide their smiles and whispering to each other as they watched the men eat.

I walked up to the Captain, happy to see he was feeling better, and hoping he might part with a morsel or two.

"You've been out with those Indian boys again," he said, seeing my wet fur. "Don't forget whose dog you are. Try this." He tossed a meaty bone about twenty feet away from me.

I ran over to it, and I was about to try this new food for myself when Sergeant Pryor came into camp pulling a whimpering Indian dog behind him with a rope. He cinched the poor dog to a stump, pulled his knife out, and slit the dog's throat.

I stared in disbelief, too horrified to even bark. I looked at the men. They continued talking and didn't even glance in the dog's direction as he bled out. When the dog stopped struggling, Reubin untied the rope and gutted him like a deer.

I looked down at the bone. I looked at the meat roasting above the fire. I looked at the Nez Percé, still smiling and whispering. The Nez Percé did not eat dog. In fact the very idea disgusted them, but this did not stop them from selling every dog they could get their hands on to our tribe.

I left the canoe camp and did not return that night or the next.

I had never been so sorry to leave a place in my life as I was when we left the Nez Percé. Mountain Dog stood on the bank with Watkuweis and waved to me with tears in his eyes as the Clearwater River pushed us westward to the Pacific Ocean.

For the first time in our journey we floated with the current instead of struggling against it, which presented new challenges and no small amount of fear, especially among the men who could not swim. Instead of portaging around the rapids, we took our dugouts down the center of these chaotic flows, which at times scared everyone, including me. Old Toby, who had decided to travel downriver with us a ways, spent the first evening around the fire removing splinters from his hands, buried there by gripping the sides of the canoe. By the second evening he'd had all he could take. He left without claiming the two horses the captains promised him for guiding us through the mountains.

After Old Toby left, Twisted Hair and another chief joined us and rode in the lead canoe to tell the Indians downriver we were coming and we were friendly.

Wood for our campfires was as scarce as game along

the river. We proceeded down the Clearwater onto the Snake River, stopping every night to buy wood from the Indians, and dogs to cook over the fires. The captains did not want to take the time to send the men out hunting for other meat. The only thing on their minds was to get to the Pacific Ocean as fast as the current would take us. Not wanting to eat dog, I spent a good portion of my evenings scrounging for food among the Indians.

When we reached the broad Columbia River we met the Chinook Indians. They crowded around our camp every night, more curious about our goods than they were about us.

Little items started to disappear from our supplies— a tomahawk, a spoon—which made the men very angry, but none more than Captain Lewis, who treated the Chinooks very roughly for stealing our things. Once again he had been overtaken by one of his dark moods, but this time he was not alone. In their hurry to reach the Pacific, all of the men seemed to have lost their patience with the Indians. The men's mood was not improved when Twisted Hair told us that he had heard the Indians below intended to kill us and take our goods.

The Indians below did not try to kill us. They thought the water would take care of that for them.

Below Celilo Falls, where Twisted Hair and the other chief said their good-byes and headed back upriver, was a narrow chute of raging water. Rather than portage around it, the captains decided to float right down the center of it, against the advice of several Chinooks who said that not even they would attempt such a feat.

Those who could not swim were put on shore with the captains' papers, instruments, and other valuable items.

"See you on the other side!" Captain Lewis shouted up to them.

It was a wild ride, but all of our canoes made it through unscathed, much to the disappointment of some of the Indians waiting below.

A wolf howls. I open my eyes. Such a sweet sound. Another howl comes from the west. I look at the Nez Percé camp. No light comes from the tepees. The fires have died down to embers and smoke.

I think about getting up and going to Mountain Dog's tepee, but I am so comfortable where I am. I close my eyes again....

WHEN AT LAST we reached the Pacific Ocean, the bad weather took some of the joy away from achieving that long sought-after goal, but not all of it. The men shook hands, laughed, and clapped each other on the back. According to Captain Clark we had traveled 4,142 miles from the mouth of the Missouri River.

Our first week there, we were stranded in a large estuary, unable to move because of severe winds, high tides, and fog. The men went hunting every day but could find nothing to shoot.

Once again we were helped by Indians. A group of Clatsops appeared at our camp and sold us food. Their sleek canoes were better designed than our dugouts and they had little trouble managing the rough water.

As we had traveled down the Columbia we had started to see white trade goods—iron kettles, old muskets, blue coats with brass buttons, even a sailor's cap or two—brought upriver from trading ships anchored in the mouth of the river. The captains had hoped and expected there would be a ship they could buy supplies from anchored in the bay. They had even talked of putting a man or two aboard the ship to take their maps and journals back to the East Coast, around the horn of South America. But there was no ship.

At a spot they named Cape Disappointment the captains gathered the tribe around them and listed our options.

"We can winter where we are, at the mouth of this river," Captain Lewis said. "We can cross the bay to the south shore, where the Clatsops say there are plenty of elk and deer, and build a fort there. Or we can proceed back upriver to Celilo Falls and winter with the Chinook."

"We've decided to put it to a vote," Captain Clark said.

Everyone voted, including York and Bird Woman. We decided unanimously to explore the south side of the bay.

"What if we don't find a good place for a fort over there?" Private Shields asked.

"That leaves the two other choices," Captain Lewis said.

They voted again, half saying they would want to stay at the mouth of the river and the other half saying they would want to return to Celilo Falls. We didn't have to resort to either, though, because we found a good site on the southern shore and built a fort, which the captains named after the Clatsop Indians.

The morning sun warms my fur and I smell buffalo meat cooking. I stand, stretch, yawn, and pee, then return to camp and to Mountain Dog's lodge to get some food. His wife, Little Deer, smiles when she sees me.

"Yahka," she scolds. "Mountain Dog looked all over for you this morning, but you must have been out courting wolves. He rode off to meet Twisted Hair without you."

I heard him ride away and thought about joining him, but I want to spend the day with Drouillard and Colter. After they finish trading, they will leave, and who knows when I will see them again. Little Deer gives me a buffalo bone. When I finish it I head off to find Drouillard and Colter.

They have spread their blankets and are setting trade goods out on them. Beads, buttons, knives, looking glasses...The people are already gathering to see what they have.

"Hey, dog," Colter says, and grabs the fur on the sides of my face.

An hour later Twisted Hair arrives with several people from our other camp. The trading begins and doesn't conclude until after dark.

When the trading is finished and the camp is settling down for the evening, Mountain Dog and Watkuweis again come to Colter and Drouillard's fire, but they are not alone. Twisted Hair and several others are with them.

"Got a full house tonight." Colter takes the red book from Mountain Dog and opens it. "The grand finale," he says, and begins to read....

January 1, 1806

Our fort is now complete. We were awoken this morning by the men firing their rifles in front of our quarters. This was the only respect we paid this important day. All of us are eagerly anticipating January 1, 1807, when we will be back with our friends and family....

IT RAINED AND stormed nearly every day. Nothing ever seemed to dry out, and the men were constantly sneezing and coughing from the damp coldness of that place. The weather aggravated my injured leg, making it difficult to run on some days.

The Clatsops and other Indians were regular visitors, bringing food and other items to trade. They were friendly, but our men were not the first white men they had traded with. As a result they drove hard bargains, reducing our remaining trade goods to nearly nothing by the time we left them.

The men went out hunting every day and brought back elk and deer, but they quickly tired of this meat, and not a day passed without at least one of the men mentioning his hankering for a slice of buffalo tongue. They also continued eating dogs when they could get them from the Indians.

Captain Lewis and Captain Clark spent almost all of their time in the little room they shared, Captain Lewis working on his animal collection and the official journal, Captain Clark drawing detailed maps of where we had been. The men had built the captains a small desk in front of the window so they could keep an eye on the fort while they worked.

Captain Lewis was unusually quiet the entire time we were at the fort. He woke up early, checked on the men, ate breakfast, then sat at the desk scratching words until evening, when he would check on the men again, eat dinner, then return to the desk and work by candlelight until he went to sleep. I began to wonder if this was what the Captain was like when he was at home. It was pleasant lying next to the warm fire in his room, but I wasn't sure I would like this every day. I had gotten used to rambling.

Whenever I could, I went out hunting with Drouillard. I also joined Colter hunting from time to time, and watched him perfect his bull-elk bugling in those thick, dark green coastal forests. He became so good at it that all he had to do when he wanted an elk was to find a comfortable spot to sit, let out a bugle, and choose which elk to kill.

About the only long excursion I took while I was there was with Captain Clark. The Clatsops told us a giant whale had washed up on shore south of us. Captain Clark wanted to go down and get some of its meat and oil to add a little zest to our diet.

Bird Woman asked to go with him.

"I don't think so, Janey," Captain Clark said gently. Janey was his nickname for her.

Bird Woman looked Captain Clark in the eye. "I did not come all this way to miss a chance to see such a giant fish. I am going!"

"Well," he said, somewhat flustered at her response, "I guess you are."

By the time we got down to see the whale, the Indians had stripped most of the meat, but the skeleton was still there. I had seen a number of whales spouting in the ocean when I was a pup, but I had no idea how huge these beasts were until I stood next to those bones. That creature made salmon look like fleas.

February 17, 1806

This afternoon Privates Shannon and Labiche brought in a buzzard they wounded. I believe it to be the largest bird in North America. From wing tip to wing tip this one measured 9 feet, 2 inches, and it weighed 25 pounds. It was a poor specimen and I suspect it would have weighed ten pounds more had it been in good flesh. We saw a number of these magnificent birds soaring above us as we descended the Columbia River.

Pomp had his first birthday last week and I would venture to say that he has seen more of this country than any boy his age. One of the men asked for a few of the buzzard feathers so he could make the boy a headdress....

POMP HAD GOTTEN his feet under him and was running around like a young squirrel, which kept Bird Woman busier than a hen with a dozen chicks. Her husband,

Charbonneau, was little help to her, but Captain Clark spelled her every once in a while so she could get some rest.

Captain Clark was like a different person when he was around that pup. He took him for walks, played with him, tickled him, and always seemed a little sad when he had to give him back to his mother.

White Feather made several appearances during the long winter when I was out rambling by myself or with one of the men. I tried to draw attention to him, but the men were deaf and blind when it came to that crow. He seemed invisible to all but me. I hunkered down in Fort Clatsop as the gray days dripped by, listening to the men talk about going home and what they were going to do when they got there. Several of them, including Colter and Drouillard, had no intention of working the land the army had promised them upon their return. Their intention was to sell their land as quickly as they could, outfit themselves with the proceeds, and travel back up the Missouri to trap and hunt until the day they died.

As far as I could tell, the captains had no intention of going back up the Missouri after they returned home. They were going to set up residences in Saint Louis, publish their findings, and along with fulfilling whatever official duties they were given, perhaps enter into the fur business.

I wondered what the Captain's plans meant to me. There was a time, when I was with Brady, that I envied dogs that lived in houses with their masters, getting regular meals and kind words. But this feeling had faded with every step I had taken into the wilderness.

March 22, 1806
Tomorrow morning we will leave Fort Clatsop. It has been
a difficult winter, but our time here has been productive.
Captain Clark has completed his map, and although we did
not find a Northwest Passage, I am confident that we have
found the most direct navigable route to the Pacific Ocean.
*   We are all eager to get home....*

THE MEN WERE absolutely busting to leave Fort Clatsop. The only thing on their minds was to get upriver as
quick as they could paddle, cross the mountains, shoot
a buffalo or two on the other side, then race home so
they could get on with their lives.

The following afternoon we climbed into the
dugouts and set off, but the Columbia had something
to say about how quick our trip was going to be. By
Captain Lewis's estimate, the river had risen nearly

twenty feet since our descent, and once again we were paddling against the current.

We heard that the Chinooks farther upriver were going hungry because the salmon had not arrived. As we made our slow way up the Columbia, the captains sent parties out hunting every day, hoping to store up enough jerked meat to get us past the Indians.

The men killed deer or elk here and there, but there wasn't enough meat left over to jerk. They ate dog when they could buy it. I survived by eating deer entrails and whatever else I could scrounge alongshore.

We had some trouble with some of the Chinooks, who were more than just hungry. Their supply of salmon had run out weeks earlier and they were starving to death. A few of these Indians were so desperate that anything that wasn't tied down or guarded by an armed man was stolen with the hope that it could be traded for food. None of the stolen items amounted to much, but when something disappeared our men got very angry.

The real trouble started when we reached the narrow chute of water below Celilo Falls. We had to portage around it, of course. The Indians stood on the rim above the men and threw big rocks down on them. A little later that same day Private Shields bought a dog to eat, but before he could get it back to the main party, the Indian who sold it, and some of his friends, tried to take it away from him. Shields pulled a knife on them and they ran away.

But they weren't done with us yet. Later that night I was wandering around looking for something to eat, and that same bunch of Indians jumped on me. Before I knew it, I had two nooses around my neck and they were dragging me away. Captain Lewis got wind of the dognapping and sent men out to retrieve me with orders to shoot the scoundrels that dared to take his dog.

"Caw! Caw! Caw!"

White Feather swooped down on the Indians, but they paid him no mind. I tried to help him by biting the Indians, but it was impossible to sink my teeth into them, strung out between the ropes like I was. I could bark, though, which I did with great vigor.

The men out looking for me heard the commotion from more than a mile away. One of them fired his rifle, and when the Indians heard the report they dropped the ropes and ran for their lives.

When we got back to camp we found Captain Lewis yelling at a couple of Indians he had caught stealing an ax.

"The next Indian we catch stealing anything will be instantly put to death!" he shouted.

A Chinook chief stepped forward and said that the two men who tried to steal the ax were troublemakers and the Captain shouldn't judge all the Chinooks by their bad behavior. The Captain was not inclined to accept this explanation, but I believed the chief. The trouble we'd experienced had been with just a few individual Indians. In their hurry to reach the Pacific, and now in their rush to get home, our men had lost their patience with these river Indians. They hadn't treated the Sioux this way, or the Mandans, or the Shoshones. Most of the Chinooks crowding around us were just curious about us and our goods. They meant us no harm.

The captains wanted to get off the river as quickly as possible and get back to our Nez Percé friends. I was certainly in agreement with this. They decided to buy as many horses as they could afford from the river Indians and ride overland, which would be faster than fighting the current.

Unfortunately we had very little left to trade that the Indians were interested in. After a week of hard bargaining we managed to buy just eight very poor mounts.

June 3, 1806
We have been back with our friends the Nez Percé for nearly a month, waiting for the snow in the mountains to melt so we can cross.

We heard a rumor today that a Nez Percé boy was sent over the mountains to Traveler's Rest. If he was able to cross the mountains, I'm confident we can do the same. We are moving our camp closer to the mountains in preparation for our departure....

EVERY DAY Captain Lewis went to the river and measured the rising level to assure himself that the snow in the mountains was still melting. And every day Twisted Hair and others told him that he would have to wait several weeks before he could proceed on.

"Still too much snow."

"Not enough grass for the horses to eat."

I hoped the snow would stay forever, because when

we crossed the mountains I knew I would never see Mountain Dog again.

Mountain Dog and I had picked up our friendship right where we had left it in the fall. He and his friends moved close to our camp and I spent nearly every day with him, learning more and more about the Nez Percé, whom I admired greatly.

Once again the captains traded their medical skills for food and other necessities. Captain Clark, whose reputation as a healer had spread, was in high demand. Indians came from a hundred miles away to have the "white healer" fix their sicknesses. He did the best he could, but admitted that often he really wasn't doing much for their afflictions.

The captains asked Twisted Hair for a guide to take us through the mountains. Twisted Hair agreed but said that he would have to hold a council with the other village chiefs to determine who this would be.

"When will we get our guide?" Captain Lewis asked every time he saw the chief.

"Soon," Twisted Hair would reply. "There is no hurry. You cannot leave until the snow is gone."

June 10, 1806
We have departed for the camas meadows and from there we
will proceed over the mountains whether we have a guide or
not. Each member of our party has a horse to ride and leads
another behind with supplies. We also have several extra
horses for meat if needed, and to serve as replacements
should any of the horses become injured....

MOUNTAIN DOG squatted down and tied a few small shells on my neck. "Be safe, Yahka," he whispered. He scratched my ears, then joined the crowd that had gathered to see us off.

I was hoping that Mountain Dog would join us at least as far as the camas meadow, a few days' journey from where we were, but the salmon had finally arrived on the Clearwater and he was busy helping with the harvest.

We proceeded on.

That night my reluctance to leave was not eased by the conversation I overheard between the captains. They had their maps spread out by the fire and were discussing what the tribe would do after we reached Traveler's Rest.

Captain Lewis traced his finger along the map. "You and your men will go down to the Jefferson River here, then on to the Three Forks, where you'll build canoes, then you'll float down the Yellowstone to the Missouri.

"I'll take a small party down along the buffalo path to the Great Falls and leave a few men there to dig up our cache of supplies and ready the pirogue we left there. While they're doing that I'll take the rest of my men up north a ways and explore the source of Maria's River."

Maria's River. The bad-luck river where we'd had so much trouble on our way west. I never thought I would see that place again. I never wanted to see that place again.

"After we explore Maria's River," the Captain continued, "we'll meet the men we left at the Great Falls and continue downriver with them in the pirogue."

"But the upper reaches of Maria's River are reported to be firmly in the control of the Blackfeet," Captain Clark said. "I'm concerned about your meeting up with that bunch. I think we were very fortunate not to have run into them on our way here."

Captain Lewis brushed Captain Clark's concern

aside. "If we meet the Blackfeet we'll be fine. I plan to take only a handful of men up Maria's River. With so few of us, the Blackfeet can't possibly mistake us for a war party." He pointed back at the map. "We will all meet again at the junction of the Yellowstone and Missouri and continue down together to Fort Mandan."

June 14, 1806
We have waited long enough for Twisted Hair to send us
guides. Tomorrow we will leave the meadow for the moun-
tains. I am somewhat concerned by the amount of snow, but
there is nothing that can be done about it....

IN SOME PLACES the snow was ten feet deep, which helped us in one way—the deadfalls were buried and we did not have to climb over or detour around them. But it was cold, very cold. The men's hands and feet went numb. The higher we climbed, the deeper the snow became. Without a guide, we risked losing our way and perishing in those mountains. The fear of this increased with every step, until Captain Lewis called us to a halt.

June 17, 1806

We have decided to retreat. There is no grass for the horses to eat. We have left most of our goods at our forward position and will pick them up upon our return. They are secured on a scaffold to keep them away from animals and are covered well. I sent Drouillard and Shannon down ahead to the Nez Percé village to find a guide for us. I gave them a rifle to offer as payment, with instructions that if the one rifle is not enough we will offer two more rifles and ten horses to the man or men who will lead us to the Great Falls....

Colter shakes his head. "That was a hard thing, going back down that mountain. Remember my horse falling? That was the worst spill I ever took. Lucky I didn't break my blame neck or the horse's."

"Potts was the unlucky one," Drouillard says. "The fool cut his thigh with his knife and I thought he'd bleed out."

CAPTAIN LEWIS stemmed the blood flow with a tourniquet and we proceeded farther down the mountainside and set up a camp in a small glade with barely enough grass to keep the horses alive. The hunters brought in a single deer, and some small fish were caught in a stream. The next day a bear in poor flesh was taken, and another deer.

This was the first time since our journey began that we had been forced to retreat.

June 21, 1806
On the way down the mountain we met two young Indians
who were on their way into the mountains. We asked them if
they would guide us, but they are reluctant to do so....

ONE OF THE YOUNG Indians was Mountain Dog! He
and his friend were on a vision quest to the mountain,
where they would fast and pray, and with luck, find
their *wyakins.* Obtaining a spirit helper is of the utmost
importance to the Nez Percé, so Mountain Dog and his
companion were reluctant to guide us over the mountains, but they did agree to delay their quest a day or
two. They set up a camp a little east of us. I was happy
for the extra time with him and spent most of my time
lying by his fire.

Two days later Mountain Dog and his friend headed
up into the mountains to find their *wyakins.* When I got
back to our camp the men had gathered the horses and

were getting ready to leave. Drouillard and Shannon had returned an hour earlier with three Nez Percé who had agreed to guide us over the mountains for the price of three rifles.

To my delight we caught up with Mountain Dog the next afternoon, and seeing as we were all going in the same direction, he and his friend decided to travel with us at least as far as Traveler's Rest.

June 26, 1806
Arrived at the scaffolds today and repacked our gear but didn't linger long, as our guides insisted that we keep moving....

Colter looks up from the red book. "I got to tell you, Mountain Dog. We wouldn't have made it over them mountains if it hadn't been for you and the others."

Drouillard nods in agreement as he translates the words.

"You fellas knew exactly how far and where we had to go to find enough grass for the horses. I don't know if the Captain's ever thanked you properly for that, but I'm thanking you now."

Mountain Dog smiles.

June 29, 1806
Arrived at the hot springs this evening....

MOUNTAIN DOG and the other Nez Percé showed the men the proper way to bathe in the pools. It consisted of stripping down to nothing, sitting in the steaming water up to your neck until you were ready to scream in agony, jumping out of the water like a boiled fish, then plunging into the ice-cold creek, at which point it was just fine to scream. The men did so loudly and with a great deal of merriment. I happily joined them.

June 30, 1806
We have reached Traveler's Rest. Those tremendous mountains are behind us....

"IT'S DOWNHILL from here, boys!" Colter shouted at the top of his lungs.

Having conquered the mountains once again, the men's spirits were high. Even the Captain was smiling—an expression I thought he had lost permanently along the Columbia River.

He told the guides about his plan to explore Maria's River, which they thought was about the most foolish idea they had ever heard. They tried everything they could to talk him out of the plan, but the Captain would not listen.

"Are you saying you won't guide us there?" the Captain asked.

"We will take you a little way and point you in the

right direction. But we are afraid of the Blackfeet and you should be, too."

Mountain Dog and his friend decided to delay their quest a few more days and accompany us as far as the guides were willing to take us. They did this to help their friends, knowing they would be safer from attack if they traveled back to the mountains in a bigger band.

Before we left Traveler's Rest I took a ramble with Mountain Dog to the place where I had first laid eyes on him. When we arrived, Mountain Dog looked up at the boulder he had been sitting on and said, "The next time I go up there I will find my *wyakin*."

As we started back down I heard the familiar call. *"Caw! Caw! Caw!"*

I turned to look and saw White Feather sitting on Mountain Dog's boulder. I barked.

"Come, Yahka," Mountain Dog called. "The men are getting ready to leave."

As I followed Mountain Dog down the steep hillside White Feather continued to call.

July 3, 1806
We have divided our party and we are on our way to explore
Maria's River via White Bear Island. My party consists of
nine men and our Nez Percé guides....

AND A DOG WHO knew with every fiber in his being
that we were heading for trouble up on Maria's River.

That night we camped next to a small stream. The
mosquitoes were thick and very hungry. The guides told
the Captain that this was as far as they were willing to
go. Once again they asked him to reconsider his plan.
The Captain refused.

At noon the next day Mountain Dog and the other
guides headed back to the mountains.

July 15, 1806
We have reached White Bear Island and the caches we left.
Nearly everything has been ruined by the high water—every-
thing but the skeleton of my <u>experiment</u>....

"The Captain underlined the word twice," Colter
says.

Twisted Hair asks what this experiment was.

"A boat that would not float," Watkuweis explains.

...I expected to leave this evening for Maria's River, but
McNeal, whom I sent to the lower portage camp, has not
returned with my horse.

The mosquitoes are terrible. My dog howls with the
torture he experiences from them. They are so numerous we
get them caught in our throats when we breathe....

IT WASN'T THE mosquitoes, it was the number of grizzlies and wolves in the vicinity that had me riled—that and the prospect of going back to Maria's River.

McNeal didn't return until after dark. The Captain was upset, until McNeal explained the reason for his delay.

"I was checking the pirogue at the lower portage and a grizzly snuck up on me. Your horse bucked me off and I landed right in front of the beast!

"The bear reared up on its hind legs, which gave me a chance to scramble out from under him and stand up. I clubbed him in the head with my rifle as hard as I could swing it. Must've hurt him, 'cause he grabbed his head with his paws and started rolling on the ground. I took the opportunity to climb a willow tree, and that bear sat under that tree until the sun went down."

"That's about the best excuse for being late I've ever heard, Private," the Captain said.

July 18, 1806
Arrived at Maria's River this evening. With me are
Drouillard and the Fields brothers. We will meet the other
men at the mouth of Maria's River when we finish here. We
are all taking turns standing sentry duty....

WE HAD PROCEEDED north, cutting across a treeless prairie. On the way we came across a buffalo that was leaking a lot of blood. Knowing that we had not wounded it, Captain Lewis sent Drouillard after the buffalo to see if it was the work of Blackfeet.

After talking with Mountain Dog and the other Nez Percé, the Captain no longer wanted to encounter the Blackfeet with such a small party of men. Drouillard returned and said he could not find the buffalo.

July 20, 1806
Very few trees. We walked along the top of the bluff, which
was nearly 200 feet above the river. Made 28 miles.

July 22, 1806
After 29 miles we arrived at a grove of cottonwood in the
river bottom. I can see 20 miles ahead, to the foot of
the Rocky Mountains. We will camp here so I can make
the necessary observations with my instruments. The game
here is very shy, an indication that there are Indians in the
vicinity hunting them.

July 26, 1806
We have met a group of Blackfeet Indians.

Colter closes the red book. "That's all the Captain
wrote." He looks at Drouillard.

"But that's not the end of the story," Drouillard
says. It's clear that Mountain Dog, Watkuweis, and

the others all want to hear what happened when we met the Blackfeet...

"We had gone as far up Maria's River as Captain Lewis wanted. We had just turned south and were heading back across the prairie toward the Great Falls...," Drouillard begins.

DROUILLARD WAS riding along the bank of a small river, hunting, and we were above him walking on the prairie. We had climbed a hill above the river and stopped to look around.

"Horses," Captain Lewis said. "About a mile distant."

Joe Fields followed the Captain's gaze. "Sure enough. A whole herd of them."

The Captain took his eagle eye out for a closer look. "Indians," he said. "But I don't think they see us yet. They seem to be looking down at the river bottom."

"Drouillard," Reubin said.

The Captain frowned. "There are at least thirty horses. If there are as many Indians we may be in for an unpleasant time, gentlemen."

"Blackfeet?" Reubin asked.

"That's my assumption, Private, and it looks like a couple of them are carrying rifles. We can't leave Drouillard down there.

"We'll try to make the best out of this situation. Joe,

get that flag out. Let's see if we can get their attention off our friend in the river bottom."

It worked. One of the Blackfeet saw the flag and whipped his horse forward in our direction. Captain Lewis calmly climbed off his horse and stood waiting for the Blackfeet's approach.

The brave was disconcerted by the Captain's reaction to the charge and brought his horse to a stop a hundred paces away. Captain Lewis held his hand out to him, and the brave wheeled his horse around and galloped back to the others.

"I only count eight of them," Joe said, greatly relieved.

The Blackfeet were mere boys—younger than Mountain Dog and his friends.

"But there may be more." The Captain climbed back up on his horse. "Several of the horses have saddles on them. We'll walk up to them, but if there is trouble I plan to resist to my dying breath."

"We're with you, Captain," the Fields brothers said in unison.

When we got within a few paces, the Captain had the brothers stop. He approached the boy who had charged us alone. When the Captain got up to him, he put his hand out again. This time the boy shook it.

Joe and Reubin let out long breaths of pure relief, and rode up behind the Captain.

With poor hand-talk, the Captain explained that

the man in the river bottom was with us and suggested that Reubin and one of the Blackfeet ride down and bring him up.

"I was pretty surprised when Reubin rode up to me with an Indian behind him," Drouillard explains. "When we got to the top we were met by Captain Lewis and the others. The sun was just going down, and the Captain said that he had invited the Blackfeet to camp with us...."

BEFORE WE MET Drouillard, the Captain had given the Blackfeet the medals he had with him, a handkerchief, and the flag.

We found a good spot to camp at a bend in the river. The Blackfeet made a domed shelter out of sticks, threw some tanned buffalo hides over it, then invited the Captain inside for a parley. Drouillard did the hand-talking.

They said they were from a large band of Blackfeet about a day's march away. They also told us that another band of Blackfeet was out hunting buffalo and would arrive at the mouth of Maria's River in a few days, which was not welcome news, as our men were near the mouth getting the pirogue and our supplies ready to go down the Missouri.

The talk lasted late into the night. Captain Lewis gave his speech about their great white father, and told them that it would be to their tribe's advantage to cooperate with us. He asked them where they had gotten their muskets. They told him they had traded furs for them at the British fort to the north.

"Ask them if they'll come with us to the mouth of Maria's River," the Captain told Drouillard. "Ask if a couple of them would like to go with us even farther, to Saint Louis."

Drouillard made the signs, but the boys didn't respond. We got their answer the next morning.

Captain Lewis was afraid the Blackfeet might try to steal our horses during the night. We were all exhausted and the Fields brothers had the late sentry duty.

I lay down next to the Captain, closed my eyes, and didn't open them until I heard Drouillard shout—

"Damn you! Let go of my gun!"

It was just dawn. Drouillard was in a tug-of-war with the Blackfeet who had his rifle. Captain Lewis jumped up and reached for his rifle, but found it gone. We saw one of the Blackfeet boys running away with it. The Captain pulled the horse pistol out of his holster and ran after him.

The boy stopped. Captain Lewis pointed the pistol at him and motioned for him to lay the rifle on the ground. The boy started to do so, when the Fields brothers came running up with their rifles loaded and cocked.

"Don't shoot him!" Captain Lewis shouted at them.

The boy dropped Captain Lewis's rifle and ran. As Captain Lewis retrieved it, the Fields brothers explained that a Blackfeet had stolen their rifles when they weren't looking.

"We chased after the Indian who took our rifles," Reubin said. "I pulled my knife on him and stabbed him in the heart. He's lying dead right over there—"

For a moment the men and I were stunned. We had been traveling for months through Indian territory and there had been some tense moments, but none before this had led to a death. Then I noticed the Blackfeet were trying to scatter our horses. I started barking.

"The horses!" Captain Lewis shouted. "Go after them, boys. We're dead if they get our mounts."

Captain Lewis and I ran after the two Indians driving the horses upriver. The Fields brothers and Drouillard ran after the others, who were driving the horses downriver.

We chased the Indians nearly three hundred yards, until they reached the vertical wall of the bluff. They ran the horses into a small alcove and tried to take cover behind a pile of rocks in front of the alcove. One of them had an old musket with him. We couldn't see if the second boy was armed or not.

"Let our horses go!" Captain Lewis shouted.

The Blackfeet boys didn't move or say a word.

Captain Lewis shouldered his rifle, aimed, and fired, wounding the boy in the belly. The boy fell over but got right back up and fired at Captain Lewis. The ball missed.

In his hurry the Captain had left his shot pouch back at camp and could not reload.

"Let's go, Sea."

Captain Lewis and I ran back to camp. Drouillard was there with four horses. The Fields brothers came back with four more.

While the men saddled the horses, Captain Lewis threw everything he could find that belonged to the Blackfeet into the fire.

"We've got some hard riding to do, gentlemen," he said. "When word of this gets to the other Blackfeet bands they are going to seek revenge. We need to get to the mouth of Maria's River and warn the other men."

They rode off. For the first couple hours I was able to keep up with them, but then I started to fall behind.

"We rode all day and half the night," Drouillard says. "We stopped briefly to let the horses graze late that afternoon. After we rested for a bit, we got back on our horses and rode until dark, figuring we had gotten about eighty miles away from the Blackfeet. We shot a buffalo and ate, then started

277

out again and rode until two in the morning. We rode a hundred miles in less than twenty hours."

"And the dog?" Watkuweis asks.

Drouillard looks at me. "We kind of lost track of him. Didn't really notice he wasn't with us until we stopped that afternoon. We weren't overly concerned—Sea was a good tracker and we thought he'd be able to find us. We couldn't go back for him, that's for certain. We had our men on the river to think about. Captain Lewis was confident Sea would catch up to us. He always had in the past…"

MY LEG WAS bothering me and it was impossible for me to keep up with the horses. It was dark by the time I reached the place they had let the horses graze. By the scent, I knew the men were a good four or five hours ahead of me. If I had kept going I might have been able to catch them by morning, but I was too tired to continue and, like Captain Lewis, I was sure I would catch up eventually. I slept.

"Captain Lewis woke us up at sunrise," Drouillard continues. "I'd never been more sore in my life. I thought we had another full day of riding in front of us, but we reached the river after a dozen miles.

We headed down a ways and ran right into our men paddling the canoes and pirogue downriver. We took our bags off the horses, put them in the boats, and floated down to the mouth of Maria's River.

"When we got there we quickly checked the caches we had left the previous year. Most of the supplies were ruined by water, but we took what we could and left in an awful hurry…"

I WAS UP AT SUNRISE, too, with my leg hurting worse than it had the day before. I limped along, following the men's track throughout the day, stopping briefly to feed on the buffalo they had shot the previous evening. Wolves had been at the carcass but had moved on by the time I arrived. After my meal I continued following the Captain's trail. It was well after dark when I reached the point where he had gotten to the Missouri. I slept again.

The next morning I followed the river down to the mouth of Maria's River. When I saw the open caches I figured the men had gone on without me. If they had, they were running with the current now and catching up to them would not be easy, but I was going to try.

I had started sniffing around the caches for something to eat when I came across the Captain's knapsack. The Captain must have forgotten it in his rush to leave.

It was open. The only things inside were a bottle of ink and the red book. I pulled the book out, knowing the Captain would want it, and I had just started heading downriver when I heard horses coming up behind me fast.

It was a large band of Blackfeet! I ran. A couple of them broke off from the band and pursued me.

As I had so many times before, I jumped into the river to escape, holding the red book above water so it would not get damaged. About halfway across I felt a searing pain in my front shoulder. I glanced down and saw an arrow sticking out of it. I continued to swim as best I could and finally reached the opposite shore. Another arrow came my way, but it missed. With the river between me and the Blackfeet, I was safe. They weren't about to get wet chasing a dog.

I pulled the arrow out with my teeth, which was the most painful thing I had ever done. Exhausted and hurt, I crawled under some bushes and went to sleep.

I don't know how long I lay there, but it had to be days. I didn't even have the strength to get up and walk to the river for a drink. I thought of Captain Lewis and the men, and knew I would never see them again. I grew weaker and weaker. I waited to die.

"*Caw! Caw! Caw!*"

When I heard that sound I used the last of my strength to crawl out from under the bush. And there was Mountain Dog. His horse was still wet from the crossing.

"Yahka?" He ran over to me and looked at the wound in my shoulder. "So, this is where the crow was leading me."

"*Caw! Caw! Caw!*"

Mountain Dog turned and looked up at the crow with the white feather on his wing. He had found his *wyakin* and his *wyakin* had found me.

"We met the rest of our party where the Yellowstone and Missouri meet," Drouillard continues. "From there we proceeded on to Saint Louis, arriving there in September 1806...and I guess that's just about it.

"Now tell us, Watkuweis, how you got ahold of the Captain's journal."

Watkuweis smiles. "If you take a close look at the cover, perhaps you can tell me."

Drouillard holds the red book close to the fire and examines the cover. "Teeth marks?"

He looks over at me.

"My *wyakin* led me to Yahka," Mountain Dog says. "When I crossed the river, Yahka crawled out from beneath a bush with an arrow wound in his shoulder. Under the bush where he had lain was the red book."

MOUNTAIN DOG brought me food and water and treated my wound. After two days I was able to stand. After a week, I could walk to the river and get a drink for myself.

The evening before we left, White Feather appeared in a tree above our campfire and stayed there all night. The next morning he led us home.

In the morning my old friends pack their horses. Colter gets to his knees in front of me and takes a handful of fur on either side of my face. He looks into my eyes and bugles like a bull elk looking for a cow. "Guess this is it, Sea," he says. "Unless you want to come with us."

I am sorely tempted. Not a day has gone by that I haven't thought of Captain Lewis and the rambles we took and the things we saw. I've thought of the men and wondered what paths they have followed. I could go with them—Mountain Dog would understand. But I feel my place is here, with my new tribe.

I watch Colter and Drouillard ride east across the flat prairie until I can no longer see them.

Author's Note

AS I WRITE THIS I am flying thirty-five thousand feet above the Great Plains, not far from where the Corps of Discovery passed nearly two centuries ago. The grass sea has been replaced by a patchwork of farms. The wild rivers the men struggled against have been tamed by dams to create power for the cities and towns built in the wake of their exploration. Sadly most of the buffalo and wolves are gone. So, too, are most of the Native Americans who helped the explorers by providing food, advice, and guidance almost every step of the way.

The captains could not have imagined me flying above them in a jet, crossing the continent in a few hours. Nor could they have imagined a nation covered with paved highways for automobiles, or trains, or telephones, or computers. In their time nothing traveled faster than a horse, and yet the captains were considered modern men. They were equipped with the latest technology of their day—compasses, a chronometer, a sextant, spyglasses, and perhaps most important, pens, ink, and paper.

The men of the Corps of Discovery could not see into the future, but we can see into the past because they left us wonderfully detailed journals describing their remarkable journey. I relied heavily on these journals to write *The Captain's Dog,* but I also used my imagination freely to fill in events that *might* have happened to give the reader a fuller sense of what these men experienced.

The idea for using Seaman to tell this story came from my lifelong love and admiration for dogs and wolves. As a biologist I spent more than twenty years working with canines in the field and in captivity. Every time I came across Seaman's name in one of the journals I found myself wondering what he thought of the incidents the captains and other men described. It wasn't long before my imagination translated Seaman's responses into the words that tell this story. Dogs spend more time watching us than we do watching them. As a result, I believe they know a great deal more about us than we know about them. A dog sees, hears, and smells things we cannot dream of perceiving. Who better to tell this story than the Captain's extraordinary dog?

As I studied the Lewis and Clark journals and those of the other men, I found myself wishing I could travel back in time and join Seaman for a day or two. I would give just about anything to see a buffalo herd so vast it takes a day to amble by us, or deer and elk so numerous and unafraid I have to toss sticks at them to get them out of our way, or a pack of gray wolves hunting in broad daylight without the slightest fear of humans.

If I had a time machine the first trip I'd take would be back to June 14, 1805, and join Seaman the day after he and Captain Lewis found the Great Falls. This was the day they were chased by the grizzly, harassed by the wolverine, and charged by the bull buffalo—what a day that was! My second trip would be back to August 17, 1805, when Bird Woman discovered that her brother, Cameahwait, was alive.

Perhaps two hundred years from now we will have time machines and the ability to travel back to witness the great events of history for ourselves. Until then we have books and our imaginations. Where will you go next?

Roland Smith
March 19, 1999
Somewhere above the Great Plains…